D0376792

AT ONCE DARKLY HILARIOUS

and surprisingly heartbreaking, RE Katz's debut novel defies genre expectations just as its protagonists defy the gendered, artistic and relationship constructs that surround them. AND THEN THE GRAY HEAVEN reads like a series of pearls slipping off a necklace—a series of stories, images, moments, songs and poems that at first appear absurd, then shocking, then brilliant, then, finally, divine."

—Steph Post, author of *Miraculum* and *A Tree Born Crooked*

AND THEN THE GRAY HEAVEN

is at once an art manifesto, heist, and road story. Here, the disorientation of grief has a surprisingly joyful orientation of its own. Katz lovingly crafts a diorama of queer kinship and artistic lineage: rendered in such detail it's realer than the real thing."

—Zach Ozma, co-editor of *We Both Laughed in Pleasure: The Selected Diaries of Lou Sullivan, 1961-1991*

NO LONGER PROPERTY OF
SEATTLE PUBLIC LIBRARY

RECEIVED
JUN 19 2022

AND THEN THE GRAY HEAVEN

— RE KATZ —

DZANC
BOOKS

DZANC
BOOKS

5220 Dexter Ann Arbor Rd.
Ann Arbor, MI 48103
www.dzancbooks.org

AND THEN THE GRAY HEAVEN. Copyright © 2021, text by RE Katz. All rights reserved, except for brief quotations in critical articles or reviews. No part of this book may be reproduced in any manner without prior written permission from the publisher: Dzanc Books, 5220 Dexter Ann Arbor Rd., Ann Arbor, MI 48103.

Library of Congress Cataloging-in-Publication Data Available Upon Request

First US edition: June 2021
ISBN: 9781950539277
Jacket artwork and design by Emma Anderson
Interior design by Michelle Dotter

Printed in the United States of America

10   9   8   7   6   5   4   3   2   1

"But I know that I want to live. At the moment, the road is reflecting this bright part of the sky that's up ahead, and all the trees have receded into this thick dark green bordering both sides of the road. And there's a gray cloud right at the end of the road and above that some strips of white pulling through the sky, and then there's this blue, a really beautiful cobalt, very light with a lot of gray in it, and then above that more dark clouds in front of a strip of a bright-white cloud line. And then the gray heaven."

—David Wojnarowicz, *Weight of the Earth*

AND THEN THE
GRAY HEAVEN

1

I married my electric dishwasher. A man with thick armhair like barbed wire came to install it in the kitchen, and I made him stay for the ceremony. I lipped a glass and then set it facedown in the top of the dishwasher, a second lipping that would seal us to each other forever.

So you're like really into that dishwasher? the dishwasher man said, touching his belt.

We're into each other, I told him.

I loaded and unloaded the dishwasher and ran it a few times in order to adjust to its new mouthy presence. The pockets of heat. The orange light at the end. I opened my arms and folded myself into the dishwasher's breath of steam.

B died, I said to the dishwasher. B is dead. It's just us now.

———

It was supposed to be me. I should have been long dead by now. As a kid, I was always sure I'd get eaten. That's how someone like me was supposed to go. No one was watching to make sure I survived my childhood of humid horrors. If you weren't trying to get the hell out of the Everglades, you were waiting to die there. I was born during the summer solstice into a place with no seasons to a woman who did not want me. I know that she was on drugs. I know that her name was Daniella, which I hate. I know that she was fond of *Betty Boop* because the one thing that went with me from the hospital was a faded beach towel with her little heart-shaped pouty face. I still have a hanky-sized snippet of it that I hold in my right hand while I sleep. I call it Boop. Obviously.

My gigantic mistake of a birth produced a second mistake: two separate birth certificates surfaced at DSS years later when they transferred me to the group home. They were identical except for the fact that I was born at 11:59 on the first and 12:00 on the second. In other words: I was born twice, and both times sucked. So, of course I have always been trying to kill one of me. Now here I am barreling into the shaky future in a tightly controlled spiral, bringing myself together in this, which is the only way I'll survive.

———

A week ago B was unconscious in the ER. For me that seemed manageable—even getting the call, even rushing in to be told that they had fallen on the concrete floor of the garage and hit their head—manageable. I was at the copy place when I got the call, and I squeezed the life out of an industrial stapler—but I did not panic. B had been unconscious in the ER before, and the next day we were eating soggy french fries and watching the Hallmark channel like nothing had happened. I'm not unfeeling. I actually have a lot of feeling—fifteen consecutive DSS reports describe me as "too sensitive (uncooperative)". And now, I have just wasted too much of my life on panic to end up fine and eating soggy french fries on the other end.

———

Seven days ago B was *not out of the woods yet,* and the hospital called their brother to get permission to release details to me on the swelling in their brain. He was out of town, so they called a cousin that B had not spoken to in years, and because the cousin had never heard of me, they frowned and told me nothing.

Doctors continue to use the phrase *not out of the woods yet,* like we all share one kind of woods, like pine trees spring from our collective consciousness with a fine dusting of snow and we are delivered there on cue. I think of my first waist-high white plastic Christmas tree that I bought with B at a dollar store. I think smaller to get to something more life-sized. I think like B. I remember a patch of fake moss the size of a thumbnail and a cellophane creekbed that runs into a perfect vanishing point. All the woods B made.

―――――

I grew up on a witchless beach surrounded by frail dispossessed palm trees. For years it was more like the breezeless set of a beach with sunset after sunset, and white noise machine waves rolling on repeat. Then the bad hurricanes came one after the other, and then it was even more toxic-beautiful sunsets to cast the pile of debris and nomadic tarp people in garish paradise neon. Either way, being a kid in the swamp was lonely. People seemed pretty busy driving around and going to strip malls and getting things pierced. It's not like any of those people belonged to me in particular anyway. I was the most alone a person can be. I hadn't even started my rock collection yet. I had no pets. I had no parents. I had no stretchy bracelets. I had a document that told me my blood type. It was B-. I thought it was the grade I was given for being born.

―――――

When the electric dishwasher arrived, I got the dishwasher man to ask me on a date so that I could turn him down.

I don't do that anymore, I told him.

What, you've given up already? he said. You're not that old.

What a thing to say.

I'm ancient, I said, and you are a damned baby.

Whoa. Calm down lady. He folded his arms.

I narrowed my eyes at him and made them into lasers. You are not even a baby, I said. You are a baby apprentice.

Like every publically shared kid in a peninsula state, I had learned to swim. I could swim crazy fast. They even tried to get me for swim team, but I was doing my own thing. I knew what other people did and I just chose not to do those things: I wouldn't do a backstroke or a breast stroke or a donkey kick butterfly but sometimes the forward crawl is called a freestyle, and I was into that.

My social worker was a tender-hearted woman with a perfect bowl cut. She wasn't naturally blonde or maternal, but she was always looking out for me. She was the one who took me shopping for my first bathing suit. I remember it because it was one of the first times I thought about what it means to have a body.

I had gone down to the public pool to swim some odd laps in my regular Wrestlemania shirt with cut-off sleeves from the group home donation pile. It was my weekly meeting day with the social worker, and she was supposed to be picking me up from the Y. I didn't want a suit, but I was her responsibility, and she wasn't going to let me go to school or hell in a Wrestlemania shirt—since there was no way I wasn't going to either. I saw her waiting on the bleachers from the shallow end. She called out. She said:

Hey, what are you doing uglying around in the pool like that?

She pointed to my oversized swim shirt. They let you wear that in the pool? Baby, even if a boy looks your way he's not going to see anything in that.

This part really bothered me because *boys*. So I said something like:

So? What's the point of a boy?

And then she said:

A boy is the difference between being alone and not being alone.

Well, I said:

I never get to be alone.

She didn't like me complaining about what the lord had given me, so she said:

Well aren't you lucky I'm here because I won't have you getting seen like that. I'm taking you for a girl suit today.

And she stood there and stared me down. She shook her head. She said:

Girl, people must think you've got a demon.

So that's when I went all demon child on her and hissed the word Ssssatan and slithered back underwater like a seasnake so she couldn't say anything. And I remember looking through my goggles and seeing the XXL black shirt slow-motion scrunching up around me like a protective walrus skin, and that's when I knew that somewhere inside there, I was a body. And people want a body to behave.

———

As a ward of the State of Florida, I was doomed to play an extra in other people's spring break capers forever. I have appeared in the background of so many vacation photos this way: capsizing in giant black t-shirts. Imagine identical bikini girls in mesh coverups bobbing on floats with cupholders. I was the oil spill dogpaddling behind them. A lot of it is funny. The rest I've blocked out.

2

Six days ago B was really not doing well. They were unstable. They were critical. They were the thing before not out of the woods yet. They were in the woods. I ran to meet them in the woods. I ran to meet them there and take their hand and lead them by the light slivering the floor out of that place. But I was not allowed to see them, and no one would tell me about those woods. No one would tell me what it was like for B who was lost in those woods.

I sat all night in the hall outside the ICU. I let them stop me, like a dope. I didn't make a scene. B would have made a scene for me. In the morning I went home and swam to calm myself down. I did laps. Freestyle, but also my own strokes with their own names. I did a double windmill and a shovelface and sometimes a coat closet. Then I went back to the hospital and sat down at the edge of B's woods and waited.

———

Doctors are such clowns. Every interaction I've ever had with a doctor has felt like an inside joke that I'm on the outside of. One time a doctor looked at my sunburn and told me it was the worst sunburn he had ever seen.

How can it be the worst ever? I said. You're a doctor.

Well, he said, you're a baked potato.

The humor in this example comes from a few places:

absolute terror at having something that is categorically "the worst ever"

absolute terror at the contrast between the doctor's control of the situation and my lack of control of my own body

absolute terror at the doctor's glib delivery of the diagnosis, which itself was glibly unscientific

the use of the words "baked potato"

the parallel structure of the equivalency: i.e., doctor-him=baked potato-me

absolute terror at realizing that to the doctor I was in fact essentially a baked potato and always would be

———

Four days ago, B was somewhere beyond woods metaphors, and I was running out of time. I didn't know that I was running out of time. I thought I was waiting patiently for them to be okay again. I was pacing in the public areas of the hospital. I was in the gift shop pretending to look at cards, and I was in the family restroom. When I got caught pacing, I moved along to another restroom. One of the nurses said that I could maybe see them in the afternoon. I asked the cashier at the hospital cafeteria what she thought I should do and she said just wait it out.

She said, don't bother the doctors because security will kick you out and never let you back in again.

I said, you're right. Besides, I can hang out down here with you.

Well no actually, she said, my shift is over.

Can I buy you a cup of coffee? I said, worried about how desperate I seemed and was.

Why the hell not, she said.

We held cups of coffee with both hands and looked at each other. I said nothing. I was thinking about how I hadn't talked to anyone about what had happened yet. This is what people have families for. I felt crushed into a fine powder—I was pigment. Blue. Windowsill blue. Ash taking air before gusting apart. No one to talk to and no reason to reach out. I didn't want our friends to worry, and I had no information or comfort to offer them.

This was all too much to say, so I just looked at the cashier's face in the glossy table laminate. I—I said to her table-face. What—she said at the same time. Then neither of us talked. She looked at the clock.

You have to be getting home soon? I asked.

Well, she said.

I'm sorry, that was rude.

No, she said. It's my son's birthday.

Oh wow, I said.

And I haven't picked up the cake yet, she said.

I love cakes, I said. How old?

Eleven, she said, grinning so wide I saw her two gold molars gleam.

3

I was eleven when I was placed with my foster mother and Ben. You'd think people would have tried to adopt me when I was younger and cuter and less of a satanist, but I was never good at being seen. I was too sensitive. I couldn't play the game. Someone would drink a bottle of mouthwash at the group home or someone would stab a pizza delivery man, and the next day it would be like, come on, the show goes on.

My foster mother ran an airbrush souvenir shop and needed daytime help. Voila: I was wanted. My social worker figured it would be a good arrangement because my foster mother was a weekly church-goer and I could use some churching.

I didn't mind church really. Just a few weeks before my foster placement went through I had even started talking to god. I was split open to god possibilities when I got saved in a car graveyard. For me, it wasn't so much learning how to pray as it was learning what prayer was for.

My group home roommate Cheyenne had tricked me into boosting car parts with her one slow afternoon. The car graveyard was spooky with its smashed windows and melted seats and limp air-bags; its disaster leftovers, its dashboard dust handprints. When the sun slipped behind our town's one hill, I asked Cheyenne if we could leave soon because I was getting anxious, and her face dropped. She looked at me out of her eyecorners and told me that she knew I was going to rat on her and she never should have brought me. She made me swear allegiance to her.

She said:

Say you're in this with me like your life depends on it.

So I said:

Of course I'm in it.

Swear you would die for me, she said.

Die how? I said.

Die any way, all ways. You know, cross your heart and hope to die. She meant it.

But my answer might be different, I said. Like I would be shot but not ripped apart by dogs.

She was just looking at me so I kept going:

I would be run over but not get burned alive. I would run off a cliff but not drown. I would be crushed by a heavy object, like an anvil, but not eat a stick of dynamite.

I hoped she wouldn't notice that I was riffing on Wiley Coyote, my painless death guru—dead a million times but never once dead.

But she was busy being mad now. She waited a beat, then she went in:

Say I can kill you if you tell anyone about this. She grinned like a mob boss.

I tried to talk but it came out a whisper. I said:

How will you kill me?

What do rats get? She answered my question with a question.

I thought really hard about rats and all I could see in my head was Templeton, who got a smorgasbord, which seemed pretty nice. So I said:

Food scraps?

When she laughed, I thought I had passed the test and we were pals again. Then she told me to take off my shoes and hand them over. She looked down at my bare feet, and I looked down at my bare feet, and I realized that I was standing in a circle of pulverized glass. I looked up and she was gone just as quick as that roadrunner. I cried out desperately. When she was still within earshot I begged her to come back. I screamed until I watched her turn into a headless speck on the flat horizon, and that's when I went silent. Sound-making is something I have mainly done for others. Quiet is for myself.

But then some miracle came for me. The glass shard ring became a prayer circle and I prayed and prayed there. I put my hands up and made one of those promises that people make in movies: if you do this for me, god, I said. I knew it worked when a group of skater kids came by before dark and actually felt bad for me, and they carried me out on their shoulders like a star player. That night I sat on the edge of a parking garage and stared up at the white pop tab that was starting to be moon, and I actually believed.

———

My foster mother was good to me. She made Spam sandwiches, which they never let me eat at the group home. She let me ride around in the bed of her truck. She even asked me to call her "mom," which I never did, but it was a nice gesture. I called her FM for foster mom instead of her name, which still made her feel good about us having a special name thing.

I liked working at the shop. It was the airbrushing golden days and people would come in six or ten at a time to get dolphins jumping over their names. Couples got matching v-necks with a burst of hearts or shells or music notes limply dangling from sunset clouds. I called bullshit on every v-neck couple. I called bullshit on romance and beach condos and Florida itself, for its promise to people who came from somewhere else that life was just one cool ad for fresh-squeezed orange juice. I called bullshit on Florida for people who lived in Florida and got heat-stroke and sea lice and picked oranges for fifteen cents an hour.

———

I got on perfectly with FM, except for her awful boyfriend. Ben had guns and dogs, and when I got home from school he'd be waiting with the butt of his gun up against the sliding door. He'd tap on the glass: one tap for come on in but go straight to your room. Two taps for don't you dare and go play somewhere else. There was a lot of don't you dare in that house then. There was also a lot of what is wrong with you and stupid kid bitch. He actually said that, kid bitch. My friends thought it was hilarious, but then again what did they know. One day we'd all grow up and just be regular bitches.

FM seemed happy enough with Ben, but I don't have a single good memory of us all together. He was one of those people who kept rage at a simmer at all times so that it was ready. He was a record-breaking bastard who made me sleep in a tent down the beach on weekends because he wanted FM all to himself, and he said why shouldn't they get to have a life together just because I showed up. He never tried anything with me but sometimes I'd wake up with him sitting in the corner of my room just watching.

Ben left FM when I was halfway through high school. I was getting ready to go to junior prom with my gym teacher Mr. Garrison, and we were trying to figure out how he could drop me off then circle the block and come in after as a chaperone. We heard FM and Ben start to wind it up in the kitchen. They fought all the time, but he had never been so pitchy loud. When we heard FM scream and a crash of pots and pans, Mr. Garrison flew out of my room and told Ben that he was going to call the police. Ben told him that he would call the police right back, and Mr. Garrison said nothing and kind of disappeared inside himself. Ben went into the bedroom and packed his hunting bag, and then he took his guns and his dogs and the whole change jar from the top of the fridge, which must have had a hundred and fifty dollars in it by then, and that was that. FM didn't do anything to stop him. She just walked out of the bathroom long enough to watch him near-shatter the sliding door, and then she went and took a bath. Mr. Garrison must have had a dark revelation in that moment because he left the house saying that he loved me but what we were doing was wrong and he was sorry to me and to Jesus. He was my ride to prom, so I took off my dress and watched TV until FM told me to go to bed.

———

Things got grim at the airbrush shop pretty soon after that, by which I mean, FM started stealing money from the register to go day-drinking in Boca—and I had to pretend I knew how to airbrush shirts and hats while she was gone.

The only thing I could freehand was a dragon because the body could be like a hose or a snake body and the face was whatever. It's a mythological creature: there is no wrong way to fake a dragon. Eventually people wearing bad dragon clothes ran into other people wearing bad dragon clothes on the beach, and they came into the shop and demanded to see my manager. I was in a tight spot. So naturally, that was the moment. That was B's cue. Wherever they were, they came through.

————

They were nineteen and tall, and when they walked through the shop doors in clean white tennis shorts and a baseball cap, they killed me dead. They walked in like they had something important to say, like they were sent by the president to tell us all who we were all going to be now that the world had ended. I shut up and the people yelling at me shut up, and we all looked at B and waited. I think B paused a minute just to make sure we were listening. They pulled their cap off and swept their dark curls back and let them bounce up in slow motion; and as for me, I watched with my mouth hanging open because I had never seen a creature feel so easy.

Are these people harassing you? they said to me, like we were friends, like we were already in on it together.

I said No, but someone else was saying No at the same time as me, and louder.

No, a woman in a dragon tank top said, she doesn't even know what she's doing.

I remember B laughing then. You paid for that? they said, pointing at the dragon.

I blushed violently.

We all paid, said a guy in a dragon trucker hat, and we want our money back or we want something different.

No problem, said B.

They moved through the crowd, or I should say, the crowd parted majestically around them. When they got to the counter, they leaned over the glass to place a manicured hand over mine.

Mind if I come back there? they said to me.

I don't know, I said. What are you going to do? It was a stupid thing to say.

I'm going to save your ass, they said.

———

B had a talent for making the room disappear so it was just us. The spell is so powerful. Now B is gone and still it is just us in every room.

4

I BROKE THE DISHWASHER and the dishwasher man came back.

I thought we went over this, he said.

I over-detergented, I said. Also I think I overloaded it.

He laughed. What has this poor dishwasher ever done to you?

I don't know, I said. Too much water, too many drowned men.

He looked at me and then the counter. What?

Raymond Chandler, I told him.

Surfer? he said, his eyes still on the counter.

No, I said, well maybe.

I'm going to show you one more time. He reached down and un-screwed the cap of the detergent compartment with great gentleness.

No thanks, I said. You can leave now.

Okay, he said, scratching his leg, whatever you want.

It's still under warranty, right? I said. In case I need you to come back?

———

Three days ago B stopped breathing on their own. I knew this not because they let me in to see them hold them whisper to them kiss their face, but because I watched them roll machines in and out all

day. Two days ago: scarier machines. The kind of machines that surround people and then swallow people whole, and then the machines
replace all the people parts and then people are just dead or machines
or both. Also, I am not an idiot. The more the nurses had to tell me
nothing, the more their faces screamed into my face, and I knew. I
could see it in the nurses' eyes, their twitchy little frowns. Knuckles,
twisting a shirt hem ghosted white. The dust bowl of their knowing.

I stopped the tears but there was something else in me that
wouldn't be stopped. It didn't live in my throat, or any other part I
knew how to close off. You always hear people talk about how somebody can just snap. People can be fine, and then just: that's it, they
snapped. But for me, it felt more like a spring—something with infi-
nite give but only in one direction. That direction was toward B, for
B; B, who was disappearing faster than I could get to them now and
faster than hospital security could get to me.

In my memory, if I really search, I can find the moment when I
actually slipped into B's room and froze, saw them or what was left
of them stone-still, tentacled, and humming brightly. The electricity in the room. B's body left there by another time and about to
return. Voices from the hall pitched over one another like a disso-
nant chord. I know that I blocked the door, but I don't know how,
or what came next. Fortunately for me, this is the part that the
police recorded for the official statement. So along with this howl-
ing hole of a memory, I get to have a notarized copy of what I said
happened in that room when they came for me just a few minutes
later. My words.

Thing is, in our darkest moments, everything we say is a lie.
It's not malicious. We just can't show up for our own version of the
events.

———

Officer on Duty: Did you enter the patient's room?

Jules Baffa: Yes.

OD: Had you been warned by hospital personnel that you were not permitted access?

JB: Yes.

OD: Who did you speak to before attempting to enter?

JB: Hospital personnel.

OD: Which personnel?

JB: Gr—::crying:: How long is this going to take? I really can't be doing this right now. I have to be in there. Do you understand? They're almost gone! W—::crying:: I've been here for a week.

OD: Ms. Baffa, please state for the record which hospital personnel informed you that you were not permitted access to the patient's room.

JB: Just about everyone, I mean. No one really talked to me much except for Lina—Lina Boorstin. I have her card here. She's the administrator they sent down to speak with me on the intake floor. She was nice, but she couldn't help me. The second day I was here they made me talk to Security—big guy—very hostile. Completely unsympathetic. Phobic, if you really want to—::muffled sounds::

OD: Ms. Baffa, I will remind you that we do not need to know the actions of the staff for this statement. Only that Security informed you that you were barred from the patient's room. Also, his name if you can recall.

JB: Yeah well he di—::crying:: Didn't tell me his name while he was threatening to physically remove me, if you can imagine. Also, the social worker down there—Brandon. I see him over there now. Am I going to have to talk to him again?

OD: Who else?

JB: There were nurses that I saw many times over the last few days on this floor. But we didn't really talk much, just enough for them to refer me back to Lina. I think one of them—a night nurse. I think her name is Carol. She sat with me. There's also an orderly I've talked to who's tall and has big glasses, kind of scowly, and unexpectedly kind. He always asks me how I'm doing. I don't know—how is this helping?

OD: Carol? Carol who?

JB: I don't know. Really? Why? I don't know. I do know B's doctor's name. Dr. Prasad. He won't talk to me though. Not once. I've tried to catch him going by a few times. I've called his office.

OD: B—B-------Khong is the patient?

JB: Yes. Un—::crying:: B is their preferred name for the record, yes. What else do you need to know?

OD: What happened after you entered the patient's room?

JB: ::no response::

OD: Ms. Baffa. What happened after you entered the patient's room?

———

I don't know what got into me or for how long, but it was all muscle. I looked at the door to B's room, now from the other side for the first time in a week of no sleep, no relief, no acknowledgement from anyone that this was my person and I was theirs; what happened was I ripped an entire dresser from the wall and launched it into the door. I heard screams from somewhere else. Looking at B, I couldn't go over to their bed at first. I just looked. I squinted. They hurt my eyes. That body, which was and was not B.

OD: What happened once you were inside the room? Did you or did you not disconnect the dresser from the wall and move it across the room to barricade yourself?

JB: I guess I did.

OD: You did or you did not?

JB: I did.

OD: Maybe you can help me out. What we can't figure is how were you able to move such a large object in such a short amount of time.

JB: What? I don't know. Grief is a strong drug.

OD: Are you implying that you were on drugs?

JB: No, how did you—how—are you just going to—are you going to charge me with something or what? What else do you need to know? If you're kicking me out, please just get it over with. This is too much.

OD: Miss—you need to cooperate with us and we're going to try to get through this as quickly as possible. I have a few more questions. We're almost finished here and then the Head of Security will meet with you to go over what will happen if you're found on the property or if you enter any of St. Agatha's facilities again.

JB: Fine.

OD: OK. So then what happened once you had sealed the door closed?

JB: What are you asking me?

OD: What actions did you take in the patient's room?

JB: Wait—are you—is B's family pressing charges?

OD: I am not at liberty to—

JB: What do they think happened? What's going on here?

OD: Miss—please answer the question.

JB: Wh—::crying:: What does a person do when the person they love is dying in front of them? What is the punishment for holding their hand?

OD: Miss, you need to calm down and answer the question. Did you administer any kind of substance to the patient? Did you touch or alter the patient or the medical equipment in any way?

JB: Well, what if I took their hand or read to them? What if I sat next to them? What if I held them—what then?

OD: Are you saying that you tampered with the patient?

JB: What? I don't understand. How many people's husbands or wives do you ask about tampering when they are visiting somebody? I know I went in without permission but—what is the real point of this interrogation? At the bottom you want to know what I'm doing here? What is the point of me? What is the point of us, of our relationship? How does it work? Who do I think I am? What do I deserve for loving B? What should I get for being alive? ::muffled crying::

OD: All I know is that I'm about to take you in for resisting, so you better come up with an answer for what you did in that room.

JB: Honestly, I don't know.

There was gauze around B's head, and their face was pulled into a grimace—like they were concentrating. They wore a single bone earring that had been nearly ripped out of their ear by the force of the fall or something since the fall, which I hoped and knew they did not feel. Some strange solace in this, knowing there were no more small pains for B. No paper cuts, no scrapes, no minor injuries that always hurt more than they should. Just quiet. Rest. There was a single dot of blood on their neck behind their ear. I licked my finger and wiped it away. All around their head, a prism of clichés. Prayers like throwing stars. No god drama here, just the wash of empty light that comes for us on the fifth floor of anywhere. I pressed my lips to their earlobe and I did the only thing I could do. I sang their song. Slowly. Quietly. A grunge dirge. I sang:

I like all the different people
I like sticky everywhere
Look around—you bet I'll be there
Hot metal in the sun

Sooey and saints at the fair
Saints alive you're saying—walk in square
The hid are out—out for the year
It's a lot of face
A lot of crank air
Eroding round here
Summer's ready, summer is ready when you are
Summer is ready when you are.
Summer is ready when you are.

5

MONTAGE. In the report it says that when hospital staff and security were able to get past the barricade, they found me lying on the floor next to B's bed. I was unresponsive. That's how they know I'm a monster.

A quiz:

Q: What kind of horrible creature breaks into a hospital room and blocks the door to quietly lie on the floor.

A: The creature who has been erased.

6

I DRAG MYSELF HOME IN THE BRASH ORANGE LIGHT and try to disappear facefirst into the futon in B's studio. It is so quiet I can hear my jeans rub against the cushion. I need the sound now: confirmation that I am here, material, real. Futon is real. Futon is all I've got. Futon is a whole medium-firm galaxy. I move the muscles in my legs back and forth less and less until I cricket to sleep.

———

In the dream I help B dream. At first I hardly move. I do not know how fragile this place is, and I worry my breath will bother the air. But I hear enormous shallow breaths: steady pulls that catch every so often. This room is B, and B has four walls. One wall is a window through which I can see people passing. Occasionally they peer in with interest, pause, tilt their heads as if they are considering me, and then they continue on. I notice one immaculate glass of water on the floor next to me. It is a significant glass of water. I try not to knock it over. Light movements. The small dance. Balletic. I get the hang of breathing in time with B. When I inhale and B inhales, the room slows to linger in its present atmosphere, images, dew. I exhale and flicker through dreams at shutterspeed. I pivot like idea. I learn to move an arm and give B a dream of horses that I blow away with the next breath. I descend into a valley. A development collects, houses on three walls. Then a dead end with an old brown rusting refrigerator in an open field. The door has been ripped off. Drop my arms and asphalt curls up from the mud like ribbon. Cross my legs and half-turn to make a sinkhole. I crack my fingers and reeds spring from the rim. I shiver the crater into a broken molar. I downshift, clench my fists, and the molar is a wraparound porch that collapses into the center. Little licks of flame over the broken wood: crackling sound which might as well be rain, and I look up to beg rain on in. Thread spooling. A green storm collects: undereyelid green. Lakewater. These are the right colors, I think. I want B to dream of their life well. Their scenery. Our swamp home. On the window wall, a face presses to the glass followed by the pad of an index finger—a thunderous pulse. The finger pulls away, taps again, and the sound breaks around me and through me. Thunder finds its way into my knees, elbows, hips, shoulders, and every part of me falls in different directions.

Hands and knees in the low light. Out of the corners of my eyes I search frantically for the glass of water. It is still upright. Completely perfect. I bend to peer closer, and I see a very small tide coming in. The water rolls itself to one side wave by wave. I wait and watch, feel all the space where I used to want things. I feel my spaces empty of longing. The water in the glass displaces itself sideways, a tidal sip forming near the brim. I place my lips there and draw in the cool water just enough to see the bottom of the glass clear. I see bubbles at the bottom. They have formed themselves into a lacework. Just then the room of B goes dark. I know it's over. But one last thing: in the dark, I feel the walls for a switch. I run my hands over the walls until I forget what I am looking for. Switchless, every smooth place I touch is a possible home.

———

B is dead later that morning. No one calls me. But I know.

———

I officially find out a day and a night later because B's family contacts our neighbor Tina with the dyed little mermaid hair for a spare key, and our neighbor Tina with the dyed little mermaid hair asks if no one could get a hold of me; and B's family pretends not to know this "Jules" and then ask Tina again to make sure she doesn't have a spare key. Tina is confused and a decent human being, so she comes over to the studio to offer her condolences.

I am a squirrely mess. I have been mostly on the futon for two days and Tina comes and wraps her big sweaty hands around my greasy head and she doesn't say anything and I cry. Then she says *I'm sorry* for a while. Probably forever. This is the first non-smalltalk conversation I have ever had with Tina and I think to myself it's going pretty well, considering.

After more crying and Tina quick shit-talking B's family to make me feel better, Tina has to go but says she'll be back.

———

Some darkness. Some light. I sit with Tina and watch the little television with the built-in VCR that's in B's studio. The only working tapes that we can find in B's pile of plastic are *All Dogs Go to Heaven, The King and I,* and a Christian exercise video that teaches you how to run fast without losing your soul. I remember when we found that video in an estate sale trash pile.

Let's do it, Tina says, and we run like hell in place while the angelic video coach repeats *Jesus is the breath within me and the wind that moves me. Jesus is the breath...*

Wow, says, Tina. I think I would go to aerobics church.

I think for a minute and I say, no. You know this is a scam because there is definitely no running in heaven.

Tina says: What about for like the joy of it? Like when you're running across the airport to meet somebody you haven't seen in a long time. Or like when you run to the diving board even though there's that no running by the pool rule.

No airports in heaven either.

But I think heaven is all that part where you run into each other's arms at the airport and hell is all that part where you wait in the security line.

So the afterlife is just different parts of the airport?

Yeah, Tina says. Unless you're a celebrity.

Next morning she comes with a gas station breakfast sandwich saying she has to go on a business trip, but she'll send her sister's kid—*about your age*—to check in on me. People have been saying they'd send someone to check in on me my whole life so I don't think about it too much. Montage. More days eat themselves.

7

BLURS ARE IMPORTANT so I'm not going to pretend I'm not having one. I have this moment maybe a week in where I kind of wake up to myself and I am actually starting to worry I can't do this on my own. It turns out cry naps are a special kind of nap that can replace everything else in your life. I have done some swimming and have eaten exactly twenty breakfast sandwiches from the gas station. I have swaddled my head in B's grandmother's blanket because B's family would hate that.

———

My afternoon activities include cleaning the pool and sacrificing my-self to the creature family that lives under the porch. I carefully skim the bugs and the debris off the top of the pool water. I send that little sucker vacuum over the pool floor. I check the chemicals, and now I'm ready. I've even smeared some honey on my hands so it doesn't take too long. Maybe the whole food chain will show up. A real event. I hope a gator will come. I crawl under the porch. After-noon happens. Cars pass. Voices. Puppet shows. The light is being siphoned out of the sky by some unknowable softness. No sign of life. I lick the honey off of my hands. A little drama is good for loneliness. I think about how my body is my own best catastrophe snack. A dark thought. Darkest. I am my darkest self right now. Everyone else is darkest thems. I crawl out from under the porch and sit on the steps to lick the rest of the honey off my hands.

That's when a face blinks into my godforsaken window of view. I squint up for as long as I can to see if I have to do anything. I feel like I'm watching the face floating on a screen, and it gets bigger and bigger until it blots out the sun right in front of me.

Hey, says the face. So casual.

Oh hi. I don't look up.

Tina said you'd be here. I'm Theo...Adan? They throw on their last name at the end like it's a clarifying question.

I am here, I say. I do a quick jazz hands.

They laugh but in a swallowed way.

I meet their eyes, and they are kind and jumpy. While they figure out what to say next, I scan them. Good clothes. Bad shoes. Then I realize for the millionth time that I also have a body, and I feel a pang of humiliation followed by a hot wave of grief, and I put my head in my hands because it's too damn much.

I'm sorry, says Theo. Do you need anything? Tina said—

No, thanks, I say. Sorry to be rude, but I think I just want to go to bed.

But I wonder what Tina did say about me and B and grief and television. I open the front door to the house for the first time in weeks and step right in a tower of mail on the floor built up to the slot, which slides in every direction. I fall down. I don't try to catch myself, so I fall hard. On the way down I feel free. Theo rushes in behind me, and I feel them push some of the mail out of the way and brace me with their body from behind.

I've got you, Jules.

So strange to hear my name.

Is your bedroom up these stairs?

Sure, I say.

I flop onto B's side of the bed and fall asleep before I can even torture myself with the dip in their pillow where their head used to be. In the deepest darkest sleep of my life, I am rescued from dreaming.

When I wake up, I feel hungover and a thousand years old. There is a crying crust in the corners of my eyes and my nose is running. I have definitely been drooling. I'm about to go back downstairs and out to the futon to coil back into B's grandmother's blanket, when I hear my name again. Theo is down there saying something else, and I'm rubbing my eyes and thinking what is this person still doing in my house. Now I'm going to have to shower and dress myself. And chat.

But when you haven't felt good in awhile, it's amazing how hot water streaming over your collar bones can be a revelation. I make it so hot I get burned a little down my back and my arms and I love it. I throw on an old Alf Christmas t-shirt B used to wear all the time. Under the fragrance-free completely generic detergent smell, there is a sharp remnant of B's smell, and I'm out. I don't mean that I faint, I just mean I'm out on my feet.

―――――――

How often do you leave your head like that? Where do you go? What do you see?

When I was first getting ready to go into foster care, I had some important sessions with the group home therapist to check on my head. She asked me lots of questions about this way of being empty and walking around. She was trying to polish me up for human socializing. Her name was Kim and she was severe, and I think from that same neighborhood where the group home was, which always

made me feel close to her despite her being cold as hell, openly ma-
nipulative, and oblivious to real danger. She drove a BMW convert-
ible and carried fancy coffees around in a collection of travel mugs,
which are the most obvious accessory announcing somebody's got
a real home to go to. She always had an intern with her, Marc, and
she was the meanest to him. If she wasn't around and something bad
happened that she could get blamed for, like that time there was a
standoff on the second landing between two kids with scissors, it was
Marc's fault. So naturally he overidentified with us, which we used to
our advantage to get popsicles or his old Nintendo—or once, this kid
Deonte even managed to get him to cosign on a new kind of prepaid
phone card someone was offering over the phone.

So the morning I was scheduled to meet with Kim for another assessment, I was eating Fruit Loops, and Marc came over and
poured himself a bowl. He sat next to me and he said something so
softly I barely heard him.

He said, hey, you know this meeting is to figure out if we can
place you.

No, I said, I didn't know. You mean, Kim is going to keep me
from leaving?

Well, the things you've been telling us about what you see and
hear sometimes—we call those hallucinations.

Like my glitches? I said.

Yeah, your glitches. And when you go "into the wall of the room"
instead of being in the room with everyone else. What you call being
"out." Those are things that would mean you need special treatment,
so you might not get placed with a family right now.

I had no idea. I was just trying to figure out how to get them to
let me go white water rafting that weekend even though I didn't meet
the weight requirement, and here was this huge thing I didn't even
know enough to lie about. I think Marc was just trying to prepare me

in case I didn't get what I wanted, but he kicked off a chain reaction in my little tornado alley brain.

So we're sitting there eating Fruit Loops and mine are getting soggy, and Marc's looking at me with that sick pity look I've gotten a billion times, and light bulb. Since it may have been my only chance to get out of that place, I needed to be less crazy than I actually was. I got that what was going on inside me was this language no one else could speak, and I was the only translator for miles around. I realized that I could lie. But this kind of lying was more honorable than lying about regular reality, since the lie would bring me closer to other people.

When I met with Kim and she asked me the questions about my hallucinations, I made a new script. I said something like, "I don't go anywhere. I just take a long time to think," and I stuck to that, over and over. In every session, I just talked about it like my head was a chill head, a pleasant head, a totally basic head. I later learned they downgraded my diagnosis to a learning disability (FM told me they told her I wouldn't amount to much in school), which meant I was probably not a danger. Just like that, I was fit for a family.

8

FROM THE BOTTOM OF THE STAIRS I can see Theo sitting at the kitchen table with a few small stacks of envelopes.

Hey, they say to me for the second time in our lives. I hope you don't mind, I started sorting. Not so treacherous anymore—they nod to the mail heap by the door behind me, the one I had slipped in earlier.

Thanks. Listen, I appreciate your help and Tina was sweet to send you, but I'm good.

They just look at me for a second and then blow right through my wall. Yeah, but how are you *feeling*?

To my complete surprise, I laugh. Honestly? Like bottomless shit.

They laugh too. We're laughing.

Also, B's brother Alvin called, Theo says. He's a charmer.

B's name sounds weird too, now coming out of the mouth of someone who never met them. It feels like we're having kitchen talk in an alternate universe.

So what's your deal? Do you just live in the area, or? I squint because what I'm feeling is like not being able to see.

Um, yeah, kind of. They raise their eyebrows and look around the room uncomfortably.

I catch myself: sorry, I didn't mean to be rude. I press the pressure point between my thumb and index finger. What, uh, what did Alvin say?

Well, he said he wants to talk to you about the cremation service. What? I say.

What even is the word cremation. It sounds too much like a dairy farm for people and (I'm maybe going out again). I try to stay, and listen.

Theo says, I think you should talk to him for the rest, but basically, it's scheduled for tomorrow.

Wow way to pull through, Al, I say to no one in particular. All the ways I wasn't invited to be part of B's living world, but now that they'll be disappearing forever, I can come on by.

Theo hands me a little slip of paper with a phone number—he's still on business, they say. Couldn't get back in time. I blink in fake disbelief and Theo smiles, and then we both inhale sharply at the same time. I like a kind of discomfort that can be shared. I don't want Theo to leave while I'm on the phone and all of a sudden am so worried that they will.

And you'll be here? I say.

Of course, Theo says. They lowkey smile.

———

In B's studio, I open the piece of paper I've already crumpled with worry and dial the number on my cell. From the window of the studio I can see into the garage. The line rings. I still haven't been in there. I can see the shorty stepladder set up in the spot where B fell, a single ominous clue in the mystery of *what was B doing with the last intention of their life and also how the hell did this happen.* Two rings. I crane my neck to see the floor around the ladder. Three rings. Four. I don't see any blood there, but I imagine it, which is much worse.

You've got Alvin, a voice says.

No one's got you, do they Al? I say back.

He doesn't know what to do with me. He laughs awkwardly like we're joking with each other.

Oh, Jules, he says with a big sigh, which feels real. How are you doing?

I'm okay, I say. I mean, I'm still here.

Glad to hear it, he says. Anything I can do for you?

It takes everything in me not to scream into the phone about how he could call the goddamn hospital weeks ago and give them permission to let me into B's room. Or maybe he could talk to his family two or five or ten or fifteen years ago about me coming for the holidays or being a totally unthreatening lovely person, who by the way, happens to love someone they love—which you think would be the best thing in the world to bond over. Or maybe he could have paid us back that money we loaned him from B's work in New York, which we would have then to buy a little bungalow with no garage where B would certainly not have fallen on the concrete floor and smashed their head open. WHO KNOWS?

I just say: probably not, but thanks.

I wanted to let you know about the cremation service, he says.

Right, I say. Tomorrow?

Yeah, I'm sorry I can't go, but I told the family, and I told them, you know...that's what B would have wanted—for you to be there.

You know, Al, that's really thoughtful, I say. My body is shaking, but I am working to keep my voice steady.

He gives me the address and the time. I'm getting ready to hang up, and he starts saying something that takes him a long time to form, so it's just sounds for a few seconds.

I'm sorry, he says. I'm so sorry for *your* loss. I know how much you—I know B loved you.

Wow, I say.

So much, he says quickly.

I, uh thank you. In the silence between us, I have a fantasy moment in which I wonder if Alvin and I could actually be friends again. Then he says:

And I'm sorry—about what happened at the hospital. That must have been…really hard.

He knows about my break-in. I feel sunburned with shame.

Don't worry. No one's going to charge you, he says. We don't think you, you know, tampered with anything.

Oh well thank god for that! I say loud and sour. And then I hang up the phone.

There is no way I am going into the crematory just because they decided I'm allowed. I said goodbye to B in that hospital room, despite everything. I said goodbye.

9

ALVIN FIRST CAME TO VISIT B AND ME when he was eighteen, but carefully watched over, and languishing in the spotlight of that real, attentive parenting. He was on summer break, and B had just a semester before started at FGCU in sculpture. We had a tiny apartment with four roommates and no real kitchen, and a gross pool shared but not so maintained by the apartment complex. B and Alvin would stew in that pool while I worked the night shift at the gas station a few blocks down. The pool was filled with brown palm leaves and dirt and some dead grasshoppers, but neither of them cared. They'd both been swimming in the Atlantic most of their lives and were not sold on the joys of chlorine. At dawn they'd come pick me up from work and we'd slide into a booth at this tiny yellow diner at the front of the trailer park where I would start my next job in an hour or two as a home care assistant. On the night between my two birthdays I managed to call out of both jobs and woke up in the actual morning next to B, a rare joy. What I remember best about that apartment was our bedroom window facing east. How we moved over each other in the mornings. Those first low orange beams coming under the half-pulled shade. Violins. A drum. Something trilling. A whole orchestra hiding in daylight.

When Alvin woke up we set the plan for the day: pack lunch for the park, hop in the waterfall, Wonder Gardens, movie, cake #1 at Waffle World (spinning case top shelf, coconut cream), cake #2 one of my home care clients (Roberta, red velvet), cake #3 with roommates (cookie cake, no one could bake).

———

Because B had just started building habitats at Everglades Wonder Gardens part-time to pay tuition and materials fees, we went for free and even got special bracelets that gave us behind-the-scenes access to tank checks! feedings! hidden lagoons! science! snake danger! break room snacks! baby animals galore! Even Alvin seemed genuinely thrilled to be there, betraying his regular skater malaise bullshit attitude. He loved the flamingoes in particular, and they loved him. Somewhere I still have a picture of him that day with his arms around a cuddly bunch of fuzzy gray teen flamingoes looking at the camera like he can't believe it. Alvin was a pretty sweet kid back then, but he had a lot of angst, and that hot anger was something his family seemed eager to sweep behind the blackout curtains of his cleverness. Alvin and I found allies in each other right away: I too was cratered with anger in a way that everyone in my life was always trying to help me ignore. Perhaps that's why that day, even though we were just getting to know each other, he felt more comfortable bringing his heartbreak to me than B.

B and I were waiting for Alvin to be done in the gift shop, and I noticed he had been standing very still in a corner over by the gemstones for awhile. So I walked over to see what he had found. But when I got there I saw his shoulders convulse a little and heard crying sounds.

I said, Hey Alvin, you okay?

And he said What? and his voice cracked.

When he turned to me I saw his face contorted in a kind of tortured disbelief, and he looked just like a lost little baby. His fingers were curled around something in the palm of his hand, which he stuck out awkwardly now that he had turned. So I looked and saw his fingers pull back to reveal a small jade marble figurine, an alligator. For the life of me I did not know what to ask next, so I just said again:

You okay?

He did some shaky breaths to get his crying back to regular breathing. Then he looked up at me with suspicion and said, look, I don't really want B to know.

And I said, well it's a good thing we are separate people then, which did not make him laugh. I mean, you can tell me and I don't have to tell B.

That's cool? he said

Cool by me, I said. Unless you know, you're in danger. I did a thing with my eyebrows to let him know I was kidding but not kidding.

Well, at the Wonder Gardens, we're all a little in danger, he said. He looked at the alligator in his hand.

So what's up with this alligator, I said.

When I saw this, he said, nodding to the alligator figurine, I thought about getting it, for JP. Because he collects them.

Marble figurines? I said, wondering who this JP was.

No, alligators. Alligator stuff, he said. He's always had a connection with alligators. They find him. And this one time I got to see it happen—when we were skateboarding, a gator followed us through this tunnel, just waddling along slowly with its mouth kind of open, like hey hop in. We weren't really scared, just it was weird. It kept following us until we had to jump a fence. It was like our own demon. So alligators are kind of our thing now too I guess.

Okay, I said. And who is JP?

Alvin's eyes welled up again, and he turned away from me. He's...I mean, he was like, my boyf—we had this thing.

So I said Oh Alvin, and I threw my arms around him. Sweet babe, we are all fucked up this way.

Then he put his hands up on my back and sobbed some in my arms. Suddenly I felt like I had a lot to offer him in the way of understanding and support and actual survival tricks.

After a minute, he dropped his arms and looked worried. Don't tell B, he said. So I assured him he could trust me.

I am an excellent secret-keeper, I said. You wouldn't believe the things I've never told anyone, I said. No way to prove it though.

Then he smiled.

And I said, hey you want that alligator? So on my birthday I gave Alvin a little gift.

————

I wonder what happened to that little alligator. I wonder if Alvin even remembers that day. This was all before he got straight and tedious forever, forgot how to talk to B except to ask for money. Then he moved to Atlanta to get a middle management seat in a pyramid scheme, a rider mower and lifetime supply of Coke Zero: see also, when we lost Alvin. This is why I'm good on people. I think I've had some good relationships, done enough caring. On top of the irreversible loss of death and disappearance, it's so strange to also have to grieve people that aren't gone but aren't here either. When what you hoped for in people replaces the people, though they are still somewhere in this world. A dotted line for family. A looking around that makes sunny days heavy. A grief that feeds on itself. Hungry-ass ouroboros of disappointment.

———

When I finally get myself back to the kitchen, Theo's not there, and there's this old part of me that flares up with big gloom and also self-righteousness because of course no one wants to stick around for me. Then the front door opens, and it's Theo with dinner, and I feel stupid grateful.

See? they say, like they know what I'm thinking.

Yeah, I say. Thanks. Feel like going for a swim after? I just cleaned the pool.

Theo falls asleep on the couch while we're watching infomercials, and I'm actually relieved there will be somebody else in the house in the morning.

———

I dream I show up to B's cremation service late and with two pockets full of ripped homemade paper from B's scrap drawer. A little bit of every color, recycled a thousand times. I hug B's parents, and they hold me for a long time. Alvin is there in a weird captain's uniform. The cousin the hospital called who had never heard of me recognizes me instantly, and contrite, takes my hands to kiss them. Then I go over to B's coffin, which is for some reason open so I can see their face one last time. There is a tattoo of a crow with its wings pulled back on their cheek, which steps mournfully over the bridge of their nose to the other cheek. This crossing means it's time. I take the two fistfuls of paper out of my pockets and hold them over the coffin. B's family claps for the ritual.

I shower my beloved with confetti. It's our version of that little flag triangle they fold and present to the families of soldiers. For us, it's bright tatters. We pledge allegiance to silence and fragmentation. We know we burst apart.

In the dream, the crematory folds or opens up into a beach. We all stand at the water to watch B's body roll majestically over the waves, then into the fire on the horizon. Right before I wake I see a crow fly up, straight up, into all that atmosphere.

10

At college, B didn't fit in with the other art students because B wasn't making things with mirrors or decoupage or self-portraits out of lipstick, and they already had an art practice that was as illegible as it was private. They were studying sculpture but were not interested in any of their assignments, rooted as they were in a rigid canon of idealized forms.

B had taken art lessons as a kid with an eccentric neighbor. Over those few years, they came to love and admire this neighbor deeply because he, as B put it, "made art like it was sex or a sandwich, nothing more nothing less" and also, he consistently confirmed their reality. Their family knew him from their church. He was in his late fifties and had been married, but he was always entertaining grad students, cute art theory twinks visiting from Fort Lauderdale for an overnight or a weekend—and these boys, they worshipped him. A couple of the boys even honest-to-god called Mr. Nguyen *daddy*, so young B had to work hard at first to decode what exactly their relationship was from all the pretentious art talk over tea. When the boys weren't calling him daddy, everyone called him V, which is where B got their B from. But B just always called him Mr. Nguyen.

Mr. Nguyen taught B lots of things including but not limited to drawing, painting, welding, cooking, printmaking, sewing, plumb-

ing, electrical, paper-making, spoon-carving, choreography, bartend-
ing, carpentry, opera, and of course, the craft that delivered B to
me, airbrushing. He also taught them how to order something in
the mail, call a company to claim it never arrived, and then get your
money back. This, he called "collecting crumbs," which was thrilling
and terrifying for B to witness.

Oh my goodness! he would say into the phone, touching the
back of his hand to his forehead dramatically for his audience (B,
rapt). He spoke slowly but emphatically, and with such silly brio, B
thought there's no way they're buying this, but they always always
did.

I've waited and waited by the door, but nothing for weeks! Now
I'll have nothing to offer my poor aunty who so loves your scarves.
She has a collection. Mhm. Well anyway she's been in bad shape
lately and we were thinking this might be our only chance to give her
a boost before she goes in for the...what's that? No, that's okay. I just
want my money back so I can get something at the store before it's
too late. Oh, of course. Thank you ever so much. Yes, I still get the
catalogue. Thank you.

Mr. Nguyen would turn to B and grin and take a deep bow.

B spent three afternoons a week over Mr. Nguyen's house, while
their mom directed the church youth choir. B's relationship with
their mother, which up to that point had been close despite mutual
misunderstanding, ramped up to a particularly adolescent point of
detonation when B dropped out of church youth choir and started
taking free art lessons (hanging out) with the obviously gay neighbor—though B's parents would insist they never *knew* knew about
Mr. Nguyen.

Also, because B's art lessons with Mr. Nguyen were so much
more about process than product, they hardly ever took anything
they made home, which seemed strange somehow only after B finally

asked for a welding mask and gloves for Christmas. It was a beautiful nearly four years B had with Mr. Nguyen before B's parents discovered they weren't just learning landscape watercolors, making a little cha ca, and listening to audiobooks.

Mr. Nguyen had only three principles that drove all of his art-making across media and concept and methodology, and he'd go over these guidelines with B at least once a week to reconnect whatever project B was working on back to the root of it. He would make them coffee with sweetened milk, and while they sipped and talked, he would roll himself cigarette after cigarette so he could chainsmoke later while working. B used to talk about this being the iconic pose of Mr. Nguyen: hunched and going crazy over a little plastic cigarette rolling machine on the coffee table, all the while prompting B to talk about their art practice in terms outlined in the Nguyen House Rules.

The Nguyen House Rules of Artmaking (or how B interpreted them fifteen years later and wrote them on the mirror in their studio):

Take a break. Lie down in what you are making.

You are part of an artistic lineage. Remember who and what made you. Make to summon. And when you feel yourself losing direction, pay tribute.

Don't wait for anyone to open the avocado. Just open the avocado.

That third rule has always thrown me for a loop. When I'd ask B to say more, they would do that thing where they ask me questions until I arrive at some personal revelation of my own, which never happened because I resisted the exercise. Open the avocado. What am I supposed to do with that now? So I guess Mr. Nguyen loved avocadoes. And being opaque. And also decorative hand towels, many of which in the Nguyen house apparently featured avocadoes.

———

In year three of B's lessons, one of the art theory boys came to live with Mr. Nguyen, and B used to say "that was the year I was born again and came out queer." Fran was a little younger than the others, stylish and ultra-confident and kind. He loved pop music and had so much to say about it, and he and B would go over and over a new album like they were gossiping about people they knew. B said Fran was like a sister stepdad to them or some safe thing that straight people don't have a word for, someone looking out for you without being expected to, that queer affection whose namelessness is its power.

Fran and Mr. Nguyen spent the summer together shouting to each other about what they were reading from different rooms of the house and drinking long island ice teas, which Fran "took the long island out of" for B. They hosted a few wild house parties that B could hear from their bedroom window and longed to attend. But there were pool parties earlier in the evening or on a Saturday that B was invited to where they would meet all kinds of men who laughed raucously and wore their shirts open and lots of gold necklaces. Men who talked to them in ways men never had before, completely un-creepy and knowing warm ways that had nothing to do with their body. When Fran was around, it was the only time B said they ever saw Mr. Nguyen soften and act like he wasn't the expert on every-thing. The way he listened to Fran talk about whatever, anything. The way he would reach up and pet the tiny hairs on the back of Fran's neck: that was love.

When Fran and Mr. Nguyen took B to see *The Bodyguard* at the drive-in, B cried into their French fries in the backseat. The three of them talked about the movie for weeks afterward. Mr. Nguyen had always been a Whitney fan, but he was worried about her. He kept saying "Whitney just needs somebody to talk to, somebody real." "But what about Robyn?" Fran said, raising his eyebrows. Then Mr. Nguyen would sing in the kitchen and do his really good Whitney vibrato, and they'd drop it.

When B's grandmother had a heart attack, Fran drove B to the hospital and "I Have Nothing" was playing on the radio. They agreed that it was the most powerful ballad they knew, and Fran called it a "top torch song," insisting that Whitney was an iconic top, and it took B years to know how right he was. When they got to the hospital, Fran helped B pick out a bear from the gift shop that had hot glue gun honey all over its paws and face. He waited with their parents while they presented the honeybear proudly at their grandmother's bedside, and all the other grandkids brought nothing and were afraid of the oxygen tubes in her nose.

11

Fran and Mr. Nguyen were collaborating on a sculpture garden in the backyard, towering structures of wood and bottleglass and iron: some things B could climb inside and some that had rungs: one dome-like metallic thing had holes on the sides for two heads and little singing chambers where voices would blend and ricochet. B's contribution was a rain barrel that would collect water and then disperse it through a system of tubes connected to sound and light sculptures that B installed around the garden, which each time the water was pumped through, would make the whole backyard scene come to life like Disney. For sound there were chimes and a kind of self-playing pan flute and even a flat stone marimba that would resonate in the rhythm of drips from an IV catheter tube that B stole from their dad's lab. For light, the rainwater turned a small mill wheel that powered spinning prisms, which reflected the light from strategically placed mirrors in the flowerbed and spun color around the pool. Mr. Nguyen's friends said it was the best day disco they'd ever been to.

When Fran left that winter, B was devastated. It was clear that there had been some kind of breakup between Mr. Nguyen and Fran, but Mr. Nguyen wasn't about to talk about it with B. He threw himself into a morbidly lyrical kind of photography practice where he would travel to campgrounds and rest stops along the highway and take pictures of wildflowers crushed in tire treads and vending machines. B later realized he was going there to cruise and then making some shots on his way out of each spot, which made the pictures a mopey filter for whatever thrilling brief encounters were calling him there. Every now and then B would see a snapshot of some man's legs dropped in with more dusty side of the road detritus. Poor heartbroken Mr. Nguyen made for an oppressively melancholic documentarian, and he made lots of slideshows that he would narrate all afternoon while B sat and tried to be supportive. B would, for example, see images like:

(slide 1) four trucks lined up with multicolor cabins against a gray sky with their drivers standing blurred in the distant background, hands in pockets, staring at the ground

(slide 2) a rainy windshield from the interior, headlights from two sides

(slide 3) a gas pump out of order, a family's worth of burger trash

(slide 4) rocky debris on a long slope down to the highway, metal netting over the rocks, with one Slim Jim wrapper stuck and flapping

(slide 5) truck tire flat with a bent nail next to it, some man's hand with wedding band tan visible

(slide 6) green wig spread out over a rumble strip;

while Mr. Nguyen monologued about cosmic innocence, the crudity of broken toys, twicelived moments (what he called deja vu), and "making a friend of horror." B learned some things but mostly just nodded. At one point, Mr. Nguyen stopped talking and bent down with his hands behind his head. He stayed like that, grimacing until the veins in his head popped out. So B reached out like hey it's going to be okay, and they said Mr. Nguyen looked up at them with this sudden recognition of how bad things were because this kid was taking care of him. Then he said, okay. Okay. Okay, let's have some coffee and you can tell me about your new painting, and he shelved his slide projector for awhile.

B made plans to visit Fran in New York while they were still in high school, and their parents found their carefully mapped directions under their bed and took their car away. Then they found the bus ticket and grounded them. Then they staged a full-on intervention. B's aunts and uncles gathered around to tell them about how much potential they had and the reverend came over to talk to them about Fran's lifestyle. Then B decided they couldn't stay at home anymore, and left for New York with nothing but a rolling suitcase full of art supplies and clothes, a Walkman, and Fran's address.

12

It was Fran who told B about Mr. Nguyen's life as an artist. More specifically, Fran told Mr. Nguyen's best story, which became Fran's best story as well as B's best story, and now is my best story because nostalgia is metastatic—and how better to honor our gay dead than sensationalize?

I'm not saying we didn't go to the moon. Fran's voice merges with B's voice in the retelling in my head. But that's not what people saw in their living rooms that night. What America watched was a carefully curated propaganda film, and yes, the most stunning piece of theater ever made. A couple of things: don't be so sure we actually did win the space race. The cosmonauts had already been up there awhile, and they were unrelenting, perfectionist. See, the moon, she's not so telegenic. Hard to get a camera crew to do magic up there in 1969, but what we did have was a group of incredible miniatures art ists, and an installation artist who was doing wondrous things with this new material, polyurethane. That was Mr. Nguyen (or V, as Fran and everyone else called him).

The story goes that Mr. Nguyen was NASA's first artist in residence, and he had big plans for building immersive installations in orbit. But instead, NASA dumped him into this project, and he was working with the American Museum's diorama artists for the Hayden

Planetarium. They were to build a believable moon set. Mr. Nguyen and his team worked around the clock, cutting wall-sized blocks of styrofoam with hot wire, melting it to shape, and painting it with a spray hose. Mr. Nguyen was the visionary behind the whole thing. He did the costuming, worked with NASA scientists to build realistic equipment, and even directed the actors in rehearsals. At one point right before they were supposed to start shooting, someone showed up with a gun and was threatening to kill everyone there for making this fake moon in collaboration with the Communists to help them beat us in the space race (Fran told B the conspiracy theory about the fake moonlanding would surely have taken off if it hadn't been conflated with this other nonsense). This is the moment Mr. Nguyen walked right up to the gunman and said, if you let these people go, I'll give you a cameo. Now that's the guy from mission control who says "Tranquility, we copy you on the ground"—and all because he threatened Mr. Nguyen. Later that year, he donated a fortune to Mr. Nguyen's work at NASA.

13

THEO CHECKS IN ON ME EVERY DAY after work at the cat hospital. They sometimes bring me dinner, but they eat a lot of greens, so now I'm healthy I guess. Sometimes we watch a movie, a comedy, and Theo fills in the dull bits with stories about Tina and their mom, and the purple house the three of them shared down at the dumpster part of the beach where they set up the carnival every year. But mostly we just swim together and talk about not B. I wonder if Theo notices me noticing them avoiding any topic that would bring us back to B. Thing is, it doesn't matter how much they try to avoid bringing up B because every other thing in my universe is connected to B in some way that flares a hundred times in a conversation.

Maybe it's because B and I have known each other since we were kids or because these are the shapes that molten grief carves in an already compromised head like mine, but B lives in everything. Like Christ. Sometimes I feel like Christians just took up the love imaginary and made it about someone with total and yet implausibly benevolent control, which is so convenient—can you imagine if the people we love could intervene on our behalf, if we could really save each other from suffering or even boredom? As a child satanist, I was suspicious. Now I'm just jealous. Who wouldn't want that god-love?

Now that B is gone, I'm even more at risk to join a cult and always have to be on the lookout.

———

One day I let my guard down a little and answer the door when the bell rings, and of course that's when Alvin chooses to show up on my doorstep trying to hug me. I let him hold me for a half-minute then I'm doing a move with my hands that I learned in self-defense without meaning to, breaking his grip. He stands there with his mouth open.

Sorry, I say. Just still a little on edge.

I'd say, he says, stepping back a little.

Well, I wasn't expecting you, I say.

Can't family drop by unannounced sometimes?

I laugh out loud. The mountain of nerve. You want to be my family now? I say.

He looks hurt. Hey, I'm trying to be here for you, he says, and B. Wait right there, I'll be right back, he says, running to his car.

He comes back with a box, and pushes it into my hands. He looks at me like this is a gift he's waiting for me to open, so I pull up the little flap and peer inside. There's a ziploc bag with a gritty gray sand, and then I realize it at the same time he says:

It's B. Well, it's some of B.

Wow, uh yeah. I got that, thanks.

My parents got the rest, and I couldn't talk them out of putting poor B in this hideous vase thing for eternity. But I scored you—he looks at the bag up close—I'd say a good two-thirds.

Score, I say, closing the box.

I hope this helps some, he says. He looks around behind me into the house.

Did you want to come in? I say, regretting it immediately.

Oh no, says Alvin, I like what you did with the kitchen. Hey I have a guy who could get you set up with stainless steel appliances for half the cost. He does countertops too.

Thanks, I say, but the dishwasher is new. We're still honeymooning.

Oh, says Alvin, looking back to the dishwasher and smirking. I have to get going, but maybe some other time we could catch up?

Looking forward to it.

He starts to go in for a hug again, then bounces back and says, just kidding.

I tolerate it. I even smile.

He waves from the car, and I wave back.

My disdain for him just feels like more loss.

———————

I take B inside with me and sit at the kitchen table. I leave them there to do some thinking laps. I do a lot of coat closet strokes because I like the way they let me go under and then reemerge new and shining with the water falling off my eyelashes. I like to get reborn so many times in a day. Each time I resurface, there's a good chance I could be something new.

Inside, I eat a yogurt that Theo bought me and think about myself as becoming the kind of person who eats "a yogurt." I feel wholesome. I sit at the table with my wet suit dripping on the tile floor and pull the bag of B out of the box. I hold the bag with both hands and some of B droops down between them. I really thought two-thirds of B would weigh more, well, not weigh more, but be more substantial. They were this unfuckwithable thing, this supernova of a person oozing idea noise and gossip. They were huge to me. Sure, their hugeness was my devotion, but it was more than that too. The biggest thing about them was their curiosity and want for the world, which I could never really share. I feel a pang, this time, of the absurdity of mishap. Mishap should have taken me. Get mishap in here. Just then I get an alert on my phone. Another hurricane warning. This one's name is Beryl. We're one notification short of an evacuation order. I should get supplies. Maybe I should run, get out of Florida forever. Get safe, if that's a thing.

Well, I say to B, at least you are safe. Something to be said for that. The safety of the dead.

14

I'M WALKING AROUND THE HOUSE holding B to my body like an ice pack, which is not entirely untrue because it kind of aches and soothes me the same. It's also a little dusty and that dust is this person I love, and I know this is why people aren't supposed to be carrying cremains around like this. I'm trying to think about any place on earth good enough for B to spend eternity, so I stop in the living room to spend some time with my favorite miniature B ever made. In a wooden shoebox-sized diorama suspended above the fireplace, a family is hurriedly cleaning up a picnic, gathering their blanket, all the while looking over their shoulders at a floatilla of storm clouds threatening.

B started making miniatures their last year of school, and their landscapes were so polished you would have never guessed that they were half-made in the silverware drawer. We ate out for two years and kept our garbage. The world smelled of spray glue and plastics glue and wood glue and super glue.

B really got into a styrofoam thing for a while. Little discs of styrofoam from so many takeout containers cut with punchout tools. Styrofoam blocks to root the plants in and styrofoam slabs for building foundations. Styrofoam heads for carvable faces with lifelike jaw-lines. The people were so fragile: it doesn't take much to make a per-

son look like not a person. One time I accidentally melted a group of
hunters into an unknowable goo and B didn't even yell at me. *Jules*,
they said, *keep an eye on weather.*

They were saying, don't worry about it. Things fall apart. Downpour and decay are a part of life, and in fact, the very things that tell
us we're involved with the world and not just here. What they were
learning to make in these scenes was frozen action, a saturated moment of life removed from the conditions that actually create life.
These bodies in motion were animated by the mere suggestion of
motion. When B painted in the photorealistic background, they used
a tiny brush they pointed with their mouth. They ate a lot of paint
back then.

But they were such a careful student of weather: what made the
sky real was never some clear blue yellow sun nonsense; but the shadow detail of heavy clouds, eerie green storm light, and sick pinks at
the bottom. Weather itself, it turns out, is just what we think of as
bad weather—anything that stirs the skies.

I am looking at this little picnic and thinking about how much
I love this family but also how much I love the storm. When B told
me *keep an eye on weather*, they meant whatever ruins the picnic is
how we know we're alive.

In the scene, the storm takes up most of the background, and
the blue-gray clouds billow with such electricity, they seem to move
closer every time I look away. B taught me about this: light enters the
eye more readily from the corners, so the trick is to put the highlights
at the back of the storm system, which in real life is exactly where
they'd be. In B's work, I've found the magic of representation is often
real magic, but more carefully rendered.

I move my eyes back and forth between the faces and the clouds,
like I always do. Fear and abstraction. Then for the first time I notice
the ground under the family. I take my finger and I lightly press a

spot next to the picnic blanket. It's not solid: it's real soil over styrofoam and felt and some other squishy organic things B cleverly used as filler. I get an impossible idea in my head and I glitch a little, but it's the good kind of glitching. I know how to lay B to rest.

———

Theo comes over with as many jugs of water as they can fit in the back of their truck, and we swim. We do the regular hurricane talk: we say hey how are you are you okay need anything, but then I surprise us both. I grab the side of the pool and ask:

Are you busy tomorrow morning? I want to take you somewhere.

No, they say, I'm supposed to work the late shift—why?

Have you ever been to the Everglades Wonder Gardens?

They laugh. Maybe they think I'm joking.

I think they're probably going to shut down for a bit when Beryl hits—they always do when it's bad, you know, to protect the animals. Anyway, I wanted to make a visit before it's too late.

Oh, says, Theo, yeah I've never been. What, uh, what do you want to do there?

Well, I say, trotting out the inevitable, B used to work there when we were super young—

Oh! says Theo, softening. They've been waiting for this moment. I'm bringing up B, processing my grief, sharing my inner world. Look at me go.

They worked with the animals, with habitats, and I was hoping to go see some of their installation work. They built some cool perches for the birds. And the tortoise. And the snakes. They made a lot of the habitat structures that are still there. They were really into that ridiculous place, and they kind of transformed it the way they did. The way they did. The way—

I start glitching, so Theo jumps in.

Okay, sounds fun. I don't really like birds but I'm up for the rest, Theo says, swimming over to me.

The birds are really particular anyway, you know they may not like you either.

I mean, I'm willing to give them a shot, Theo says.

No, probably best to stay away. They can sense it. They will feel your antibird sentiments.

Theo gives me a look.

I slip under the water like a big hand came from above and pushed me. I go all the way to the bottom and pull my knees up to my chest. I open my eyes and the pool lights make the water blue in a way that is more than blue: cerulean. Cerulean, I think. Cerulean cerulean cerulean. The word itself is deoxygenated. This blue is holding its breath.

When I resurface, Theo says, hey. You know what I'm excited for tomorrow?

What? I say, wiping my nose.

Well birds, for one thing.

That's the spirit.

When Theo was a kid, they tell me, they would leave their house after Tina and their mom and their mom's girlfriend were asleep and walk around the carnival. It was only a block from their house and bright enough to light up the entire shoreline. When they kept showing up night after night the guys who worked the entrance started letting them in for free, and they would hang out at this one game stand where people would have to shoot the little rubber frogs into lily pads. When they learned how hard it was to win a top row giant stuffed animal prize, they stopped believing in luck and realized that so much of the world moved like those lily pads. The game wasn't broken, it was just rigged by one person with hand controls and people were just hopelessly flinging those stupid little frogs all night thinking *somebody's got to win right? It could be me—why not put another dollar down?* After games, Theo would ride the ferris wheel by themself, even though they weren't quite tall enough, and they'd look down at their house looking just like a dollhouse with the little porchlight on and have this dangerously zoomed-out perspective for a kid with no way out of that neighborhood. The last thing they always did before going back to bed was hike up their pajama pants and walk carefully along the surf, shepherding any baby sea turtles dazed by the carnival light back to the water. Even so, Theo says, the birds would find a way to snatch up a few at sunrise. They wouldn't tell me how they knew, but I understood what they wanted me to understand about birds.

15

B's PART-TIME WORK at the Everglades Wonder Gardens was a way of leaning into a lifelong curiosity about the natural world, which they had engaged with only in the suburban apocalyptic sense. Every road in their town, pavement or gravel, or mud, led to barbed wire wasteland and then just beyond: swamp, nasty embankments and viperous groundcover. And then there were the finer touches of the post-industrial landscape: marked dog graves in a sacred semicircle around some high voltage transformers. These were the vistas of my childhood as well, but I was farther from the ocean, and farther still from the safety of resting my head on the backseat window of the family minivan, which is to say, I could not relate to B's urge to push into the wild. I was a feral child. B had bunkbeds and a basement game room and one carefully groomed poodle. Remarkable what ripens in the young headspace of imagined other lives: they wanted wilderness the way I wanted my own bedroom.

The flora and fauna of south-central Florida are a colorful lot: spindly, poisonous beauties that thrive in humidity and sawgrass and garbage. Despite everything, I have always felt at home among them.

Come to Florida! We have sixty kinds of orchid! We worship mating pairs of bald eagles and other symbolic birds! Come to Florida: you will only get blown over a little, burned a little, bitten a little. Florida has a reputation for being both uninhabitable and too overgrown with life. But make no mistake: the precarity of the peninsula is white settler legend. The land is hostile because it is good at fighting for itself against invasion. All of the venom of Florida is purposeful. When Europeans first took Florida from the Seminole and Miccosukee people, they found they had to do a lot of work to make it comfortable, or more specifically, that they didn't know how to live in Florida because they were not supposed to be here. Basically, they got here and immediately regretted it, which did not mean they stopped being greedy and murderous, but just that they didn't want what they'd stolen and looked for greedy and murderous ways to offload it. It goes like this: after hundreds of years of colonial violence, the Spanish handed over Florida, a "neglected colony" to Great Britain. A few years later, the British returned Florida to the Spanish because they couldn't handle the elements. These callow conquerors, they fled the weather.

———

Because B was trying to get closer to the animals and plants native to Florida, working at the Wonder Gardens seemed like a good way to do that while still maintaining the ironic detachment of an art student. At first they had to perform a rotation of low-level roles at the Gardens, including cleaning up after the animals, which for the two weeks they did it around the clock, threw them into a full existential panic. Nothing like standing around waiting to catch animal shit to really put you in your place. I comforted them, and then gently reminded them that some people do this work all their lives, at which point they looked at me with full-blown middle-class horror. Then the guilt would bubble up and they'd reassure me that I wouldn't have to do home care forever, and I would say for the millionth time,

I actually don't mind it. Even now, when I think back: I've had some of the best conversations of my life while cleaning up shit.

After scrubbing tanks and picking up soggy gator pellets for their last training rotation, B had racked up a few ideas about how to improve the animal habitats. They thought, given their extensive construction experience under Mr. Nguyen, the Wonder Gardens might be open to their renovations. Occasionally the owner of the Everglades Wonder Gardens would run a staff meeting for that family farm feeling, and B kept plans in their locker in preparation for that moment. When there was a special staff meeting to address the gator incident with a tour group that had to run for the exits, B was ready. Following the meeting, they pitched a construction project in the parrot house that could be replicated for the other bird habitats. B's plan was to build swinging, tiered perches that allowed for better visibility for Gardens visitors while also creating more space for the parrots to actually fly in between resting periods. B also proposed replacing the lower section of the roof with a hanging lattice that acted more like a forest canopy, which shimmered with the fake fan winds that guided the parrots' coasting movements.

B used old reptile habitat materials the Gardens already had in a storage shed, and many of the parrots were more active and healthy than they'd been in a long while. Crowds began to gather in front of the bird habitats again. B and their supervisor gave a presentation on the success of the project, and B remembers the Wonder Gardens owner, a particularly entrepreneurial descendent in the Wonder Gardens dynasty, smirking at them in a way that they swear they saw little cartoon dollar signs pop up in her eyes. B was promoted to habitat restoration. Within a year, they were heading up the department.

16

B's SCHOOLWORK HAD TAKEN A REAL DIVE: they were on track to graduate but could not find anyone to chair their thesis committee. They had refused the recommendations of three different professors, which amounted to a chorus of concerns about measuring technical proficiency in a particular medium. B had made a collection of objects they felt spoke to one another, and no two shared a material ancestor. The centerpiece of their exhibition was a masterfully detailed diorama of a circle-jerk scene in a dingy attic with peeling floral wallpaper. Depending on how carefully people looked, they would be scandalized or barely notice. The move was so midtwenties of them, it kills me.

Just weeks before their solo show in the University gallery, they asked for my help completing the artist statement they had been avoiding.

Okay, I said, give me some terms that you would use to describe your work.

Like all of my work? said B.

Yes, your body of work: just some unifying themes or, is there a way you'd group each object in your show together?

See this is why I haven't come up with a title for the show yet.

You're going to have to send it to the vinyl place for gallery text this weekend anyway, so now's a good time to figure it out. Just tell me what you've been thinking about while making your show this semester.

Okay. B took a deep breath and closed their eyes. They opened one eye, like a reverse wink. Ready?

I'm ready!

They said: post-conceptualisms.

I rolled my eyes: NEXT, I said.

Hypermaterialism.

Fine.

How exploring othered lives, no matter how careful, is a busted process. Fetishized labor plus good ol' fear of annihilation.

Okay, now we're getting somewhere.

But like the dream-version of fear. The unfearsomeness of that fear. Deterritorialized identity. Why I'm donating my body to science.

Why again are you donating your body to science?

If I were going to take up my birthright and do myself in, they said, pausing (B's grandfathers on both sides had ended their own lives, which they casually referenced far too often). It'd be a murder-suicide because my brain came from somewhere else and will go back to that alien place and the world can have my body for cuttings and sweetmeats, small life they go on bringing.

You're a fanatic, I said. Are you your brain or your body?

B thought for a second. I wish I were my body.

Me too, I said. Maybe some people are.

Will you hold my hand? they said suddenly, reaching out.

Sure, I said.

B was such sweet nonsense. At the end of this exercise, I ended up just asking them for their perfect shopping list for the show: what real or imaginary materials would they have sought out or purchased if they could have every little thing they needed.

The artist statement I wrote for them read:

For this show, B Khong would have liked to give you everything. Please help yourself by imagining these objects they specifically meant to pick up but did not have time:

half-used birthday candles

an oversized calculator

fists cast from fists

postcards from the interior of a small (unlocatable) room

play bricks

wicker toys

twins

a memory game

candy cigarettes

a wolf mask

a garlic press that cannot be unpressed

tenterhooks

an unnameable mineral oil

a stack of paper hats

"nun things"

baskets so large everything in the world sifts through

magnetic tape

fishnet stockings ripped at the crotch

the sound a hearing aid makes when it runs out of battery

mines both flooded and on fire

a cut leather belt

a mountain with a zipper up the back

safe assumptions

some blue octagons

a honey spoon

a little drink umbrella over a sewer grate
data visualization software
"more purples"
a lightbox
fermented fruit
a teardrop-cut ruby
endangered dunes

17

THEO AND I PACK THE TRUCK midmorning to drive to the Wonder Gardens. Before we get an hour out, we pass a peach stand and an egg stand and a boiled peanuts stand, and each time Theo hops out of the truck and jogs over to the spoils with an enthusiasm I cannot decipher.

What's so exciting about boiled peanuts? I finally say.

There just aren't a whole lot of places you can buy stuff from local farmers anymore. I love them.

I mean I like boiled peanuts just as much as the next person, but they're nothing to write home about.

I love the farmers, they say, sneering.

Oh that's right, you come from farm people.

Theo says: what kind of people are your people?

I don't know, I say. Moonshine people probably.

Moonshine people are farm people, basically.

Or something really boring: railroad people? Shoe people? Cement people?

I wouldn't trust you with cement, Theo says.

Yeah, I really shouldn't be pouring sidewalks. I'm not cut out for public consumption.

Maybe railroad people. I can see you riding the rails, dropping into places for a day or two and looking around. Maybe you stay in a small town and befriend some folks and solve all their problems before you leave. Like in those movies, all those movies. You could change your name every day. Theo makes a waving motion with their hand.

I do love being different people. Different helpful people.

Yeah, because you're a Gemini-Cancer cusp baby.

What does that mean?

What should we have for lunch?

I don't know. Whatever you want, I say.

That's your Libra, Theo shouts, cutting the wheel sharply to the left into a driveway I didn't know was there. A little yellow cottage with a hand-painted sign that says "UGLY PICKLE".

What is this place?

They have fantastic sandwiches, says Theo.

But I don't know which birth time is right.

It's the Libra one, says Theo, touching my elbow.

They walk toward the cottage, and I'm thinking oh no, I'm going to start caring about astrology now.

————

When we get to the Everglades Wonder Gardens, there is a summer camp going on and I realize I'd forgotten about the summer camp B created for middle school students to explore animal ecosystems. B wanted to lead the kids through actual marshlands and wade through shoals, but the Wonder Gardens was too worried about liability: they had already had some close calls on the grounds, and it seemed like all they needed was for one overeager kid to tumble into the muck like Augustus Gloop and it'd all be over.

Theo and I look over the Gardens map and made a quick list of the places we absolutely must see, with a few honorable mentions if we have time.

In the order of necessity: parrots, snakes and reptiles, alligators, turtles, butterfly garden, flamingos, petting zoo, bromeliads, gift shop.

Theo figures it's only fair that if we see the parrots, we have to spend some time with the turtles, which is fine by me. The alligators are essential for first-timers, so we buy some pellets. I give them the warning the tour guides give about how close the alligators get, and how they're so used to people by now they're bored but careless. I also tell them about the exhibit that's just a gold watch in a case, a gold watch that saved the left hand of one of the Wonder Gardens scions at feeding time years ago. I'm watching the time to make sure we get to the butterfly garden because it is a strategic place to tell them about my plan.

The parrot house is exactly as B left it, and their latticework ceiling shimmers like a forcefield over the bright parrot heads and enormous fronds. There's a tiny plaque next to the glass that mentions B's renovations, but does not mention them by name. At first I'm upset, but then I realize that the plaque would deadname them forever, so it's best this way. Collective memory is complicated for us. When we die, do we belong to only those who remember us as we knew ourselves? I would say we do, but that's not what history is.

Theo lights up when we get to the turtles, and it's like the boiled peanuts all over again. They are mysteriously excited about so many things, I'm starting to wonder if I'm just so accustomed to being unexcited I'm the one who's off. Then we get to the butterfly garden and I get nervous because I'm going to have to let Theo see really see me, see my grief and desperation and beyond that, what I'm capable of. The raw lunacy of my scheming. What I would do for B.

We're watching a blue iridescent butterfly alight on a few overripe slices of pineapple, and then a tiny white butterfly lands right on my hand. I lean in to get a closer look and for a second it seems like the butterfly is making a facial expression with its actual face. I think *does this butterfly know something*. Then an identical tiny butterfly lands on my other hand, then a third lands on my shoulder. Theo is laughing.

Hold still, they say, holding up their phone.

Wait, I say. How's my hair.

Cute, they say, and they run their fingers through my front curl once and take the picture.

The butterflies are still with me, and I feel their quiet power. I say, hey Theo.

Yeah? Theo says, swiping through the pictures they've been taking.

I was wondering if I could borrow your truck. For like, a few weeks.

Theo lowers their phone and looks sideways at me. Going somewhere? they say.

The butterflies lift off and round each other like skywriting, and I am looking for the message.

Jules, Theo says.

I have a plan, I say. I need to do something, for B. It's kind of big and kind of illegal. Very illegal. But I've been doing some research and—

Okay, wait, Theo says, dropping their phone into their shirt pocket. Tell me everything.

Maybe you should sit down, I say.

———

So, Alvin came by the other day.

Oh wow, they say. Everything okay?

He dropped off some of B's ashes, I say.

Theo makes a little O shape with their mouth. O-okay, they say. Some?

Yeah, I say, just some.

I go over the basics, that B worked in a lot of museums over the past fifteen years. I tell them: there were a few projects they really loved. Big career-making moments, and more than that, places they were really happy. Gainesville, Chicago, New York, I say.

Gainesville? they say back.

Their first job, I tell them, and well, I've never even been to Chicago.

They're giving me this worried look, then they look pained, and by the end they're sitting next to me with their elbows on their knees, reeling. They are trying to wrap their head around this demon idea, so we're doing a call and response thing: three museums, two weeks, they say to me.

And this ground, it's softer than real ground, I say back.

Three museums, says Theo. You want to bury B in these places they made.

Right, I want to bring them home.

They look up at me with the same glint in their eye now, and they say: where they can really rest.

I smile. No weather, I say.

18

THE SUMMER AFTER B GRADUATED FROM SCHOOL, we visited Fran in New York. They hadn't seen him since they stayed with him after dropping out of high school. They left their parents' house and caught a ride to New York because they had already been trying desperately to visit Fran when their family discovered they'd been sleeping with a girl from art class and doubled down on isolating them from their friends and the world. Fran had taken them in and, among offering other points of access (club kids, the art underworld, and well, drugs), set them up with a mattress on the floor and a GED class right in Harlem.

Fran invited us back to celebrate B's college graduation with him in Fire Island, and I had never been invited to do anything so gay out in the blaring light of day. This was more B and Fran's world than mine. I had been to smalltown gay bars where butches and femmes paired off to slowdance around pool tables. Even the few times I had been to drag shows up in Savannah, or clubbing in Miami, I didn't know who I was supposed to be, how I was supposed to dance. By my second night in Fire Island, I wandered away from the men in thongs playing volleyball and hipster bars, and found a group of women down the beach who called out to me. They said I looked lost and offered me a seat in their chanting circle. We did a little chanting, but mostly we just talked about Chelsea and film and the ocean and how disappointing it was that all the art queers were corporate jocks now. Their trans press was holding a retreat for a month on an artist grant, and they were tired of the whole scene by day one. I spent the rest of my nights at their fire, feeling something in me seen for the first time. When I would get back to Fran's place at whatever time, he and B would be talking about some surreal adventure they'd just been on, and Fran would feed me something and say, *having a good Fire Island baby?*

Maybe it took me awhile to arrive to myself, and at such a silly gay resort, but it felt like the beginning of my real life, and by that I mean not who I was or am (which I've always known), but who I belonged to. There were people who not only saw me but wanted me, and not because we were the same, but because no one was the same and it was exhausting to live always trying to make it all fit.

———

When B and I got back from New York, there was a message on the answering machine from the Florida Museum of Natural History. That Wonder Gardens heiress who had been so taken with B's parrot house recommended B to a family friend in museum development. She heard they were looking for an artist who knew the South Florida landscape to do painting and restoration in the People and Environments exhibits, and that was B's ticket (and my ticket) out of the swamp.

It was strange to move to the dead landlocked center of a state so defined by the Atlantic, and even stranger to leave the suburban swamplands of our childhoods so that B could rebuild them in an air-conditioned exhibit hall for people to look in on. The Everglades defied observation: that is, they were impossible to watch because there was no place to stand where you were not immersed in their wetness, that wild bog life taking your creature body way back in time. In the Everglades, you sweat a sweat that redistributes you to the land. That's what it's for.

———

B started at the Florida Museum before we were even fully moved into our place in Gainesville. They spent their days learning how to restore a life-sized mangrove forest while I worked as a personal assistant through University of Florida and a server at a bed and breakfast on the main strip. We didn't have a lot of furniture, and were driving around in the evenings looking for couches on the curb or dresser drawers next to a dumpster. Some of my clients donated kitchenware, a nightstand, and an old organ with stuck pedals that B would play Queen songs on for the neighbors every Sunday morning like our very own queer church service. One client gave us a brown recliner, and B would sometimes fall asleep stretched out in it reading up on the history of the Everglades, which we knew but didn't know because the education system had failed us by trying to make us feel kindred with colonial ambition. The American dream had already variously soured for each of us, so we were bad history students and good shit-stirrers.

In addition to repainting the freshwater pools of South Florida, B was doing some shit-stirring in the fishing gallery at the Museum. They were starting on a restoration of clay huts and figures illustrating the Calusa people fishing the estuaries. Nowhere in any of the gallery text did the Museum acknowledge how exactly the Calusa and Tequesta peoples had been annihilated, or even how the Seminole came to be a diverse alliance of escaped slaves and tribes pushed into the Everglades by the U.S. military. B would sometimes act out by sneaking in a particular anachronism meant to unsettle museum visitors, like a sculpted clay can of Bud Light in a Calusa chief's hand, or an oil spill in the background of a miniature demonstrating the use of fishing nets.

They were able to get away with it because they were starting to get attention in the industry; but they were quickly moved along to restorations in the Northwest Florida: Waterways and Wildlife exhibits where they wouldn't be tempted to be "political" (*as if the earth were ever apolitical,* B used to say). While they worked on the hammock forest and marshes, other restoration artists would take notes. People came from larger museums to observe their foreground plant techniques. They could paint around an irregular curve in the background scenery and use color so hyperreally, it was like standing inside somehow staring at a distant horizon. They were known for their understanding of weather patterns, their clouds like wheels that made the still skies move. And they had a special thing they could do with lighting design that made the sun seem like it was bursting through the clouds for this one specific moment on the forest floor.

In real life, B knew how to find the light too. They would just be making lunch or pulling weeds from the garden or talking—saying something smart but morose about the nature of the human soul, like how we don't know what it does so it's possible that it's anywhere doing anything. Look out, your soul is working at the plastics factory! Or whathaveyou—saying something ludicrous but compelling, and this beam from somewhere would find their face and shred the shadows around us.

19

THEO IS GOING TO LET ME USE THE TRUCK on the condition that I stop pretending like I can do something like this on my own and ask for help. They have some vacation days coming up anyway, they say.

Okay, I say, but I'm not getting you arrested. I go in alone.

I wouldn't take that from you, they say, and I know they get it.

But maybe we can get some walkie talkies for while I'm in there, I say.

You know we have smartphones now, right?

Yeah, but they can't put a wiretap on a walkie talkie.

No one is trying to wiretap your ass breaking into a museum to not even take anything, says Theo, giggling.

This is why Theo's good. Even when they're making fun of me, I feel comforted.

———

We take the weekend to plan. We lay out maps of each museum over the kitchen table like we're staging a heist with some kind of vault situation at the end. I think about being the person who gets into the vault but can't get out. The staged world can have me too.

We pack camping supplies, emergency food and water, clothes, books, travel guides, and I tuck B into an old army backpack they used to take on their research trips. I cover the pool and take some of the more fragile plants inside.

I am trying to call the hurricane by their proper name. Seems to me the proper name of a hurricane is probably in a language made of golf-ball sized hail, so we can't ever know what a hurricane calls themself. But I know Beryl is powerful, and I submit. I also know Beryl is supposed to go right over this beach on Tuesday, so I'm planning to be in a day in Gainesville by then. It turns out beryl is a kind of emerald that can be used to protect travelers, so that feels important. And I read somewhere that an Italian warlock named Pliny the Elder used beryl to cure diseases of the heart, which I'm thinking would include gutted by grief to the point of felony. We eat dinner with Tina and tell her as much information as we can without telling her where we're going or why. She thinks we're having some kind of carefully planned (by which she means gay) tryst, which funnily enough reminds me to call the dishwasher man one last time.

———

Can you come before Beryl gets here, I ask him over the phone.

The hurricane shouldn't affect your dishwasher unless your electrical goes out, or well I guess depending on the flooding.

I just want to make sure everything is working properly. I want you to know this will be the last time I call.

Are you breaking up with me, he says, with an awkward laugh.

I prefer to do these things in person, I say.

Oh no, wow he says. Okay, how's 8?

When he arrives, he checks the filter and the little computer and tests the rinse and dry cycles.

All good here, he says, wiping his hands. I never noticed the tattoo on his calf before: two men on their hands and knees. One man is holding their other man down with his whole body and they are both grimacing with pain, or pleasure, or both.

Are they fighting or fucking? I say, pointing.

The dishwasher man blushes up a storm when I say this and shouts, what?! He spins around, trying to look at his leg to figure out what I'm seeing. He says: they're wrestling. Jesus, they're wrestlers. I love—I mean, I coach, wrestling at the high school.

Then I say, I think it's time we moved on.

Wait, he says.

I say: me, the dishwasher, you.

But, he says, touching his belt. I mean, you still have a warranty.

I hope this doesn't break your heart, I say, and I mean it.

———

When a hurricane is on the way, people remember how to do the magic of listening. They talk to their neighbors, read the rustling leaves, look up and up and up. I do a little air and water spell to ask Beryl to be gentle with them.

Theo drives the first leg because they know the good shortcuts to avoid the tourist traffic this time of year, though we realize quickly many tourists have gotten the message and are vacationing north. The roads are desolate, and the sky is already that hurricane yellow with heavy pulls in every direction like a new kind of gravity. B rides shotgun with me, and although this is already our quietest family trip, I can hear them. I can hear them laughing about me going back to Gainesville for this.

Theo asks me: So what did B like to do in town?

Oh you know, we had a pizza place. They used to go to this used bookstore all the time. Uh, there's a decent drag scene, karaoke, lots of places to swim and be in nature. UF stuff, museums.

Well we'll definitely see a museum or two, they say.

Cute, I say. Sounds like a blast.

But is there anything else you want to do while you're here?

You mean, like in memoriam?

If that's what you want to call it. Or just, places and memories to reconnect with.

There is one spot I can think of.

———

We get to the Super 8 off I-75 and drop off our stuff before heading to the museum. Theo has plans to pay in cash and use their mom's name at the desk: *we need to call in all our ghosts for this one,* they say. We scope out the continental breakfast area, which is my favorite part of motel life, and this one looks pretty good. They have catering trays for hot food, a juice machine, a little fridge with yogurt cups and milks, and three waffle-makers: luxurious. I wonder about Daniella and if she would be any help. I wonder about all my ancestors and whether they keep track of me or even know to wonder how I'm doing. Blood family always seemed overrated to me, but it's good to imagine someone out there with karmic clout when things feel messy.

The Florida Museum is packed with groups of camp kids all wearing the same t-shirt, gigantic strollers, and sunburned people in bucket hats. Theo and I enter separately two hours before closing as we planned. I have an hour to inspect B's hammock forest and check on access, terrain and floor plants, lighting, camera location, and any other potential problems. Then I'll meet up with Theo in the butterfly rainforest to verify my hiding spot is completely hidden from the aerial camera and other viewpoints. After debating all morning about what colors I should wear, and I end up going with green shirt black pants. When I see some young goths by the waterfall, I'm grateful for their whole seasonally inappropriate, unfriendly vibe. I pretend to do some intense birdwatching and sidle up close as I can get to my actual hiding spot while Theo uses their phone to inspect the live webcam. Then they move all around the room, checking every hole in every leaf for a glimpse. There are fewer cameras in this part of the museum because of the canopy camera, which is blocked in many places by massive ferns; and there is little regular custodial work in here. After the botanical and wildlife staff close up for the night, it's just a sleepy indoor rainforest.

There is good night security here, but Theo managed to snag their rotation schedule on their way back from the bathroom, so we know when they'll be in which rooms and for how long. Once I bury B, I retreat to the staff administration area that's closed to the public, where there is only one security rotation at midnight. I leave with the first shift out that back door, when the alarm is reset until morning. Theo is waiting with the truck across the street at the Hilton. This is the plan, and it's near-perfect for a weekend of planning, a few hours in the museum, and two and a half viewings of Oceans 11.

They make the museum closing in ten minutes announcement, and Theo gives me a long hug.

Don't fuck it up, they say, rubbing my shoulders.

I feel like I'm about to cry, but I swallow it and snort-laugh instead. I tell them: if I don't make it to the Hilton, remember me brave.

20

In the Hilton parking lot, Theo is so happy to see me they scream, but I'm breathing hard and sobbing. I'm covering my face because I am eaten by shame and I can feel Theo looking between my fingers to find my eyes.

What's wrong what is it? they say.

Notice anything missing? I say, holding out my hands. I show them my back.

Oh my god, they say. No.

I had to leave B there.

Wait, did you—

Yeah, it's done, I say. But then one of the guards was early, and I couldn't reach the bag. I barely made it out as it was. The whole time I was standing there waiting for first shift to leave, I was trying to figure out how to get back into the hammock forest to rescue them.

Okay, where is B?

They're behind some logs and underbrush near the corner of the background painting. My breathing has slowed a little and I can think. I realize it's an army backpack, so camouflaged as if for this strange purpose.

Don't worry, Theo says. We'll get it tomorrow.

I nod, grateful not to have to hide this time.

Think of it as an addendum to the plan, they say, which worked pretty well, right?

I'll count it as a victory when we get B out, I say.

———

Back at the Super 8 I've been tossing and turning in our squeaky queen bed for what feels like hours, and I nearly jump out of my skin when Theo starts talking without opening their eyes or moving at all.

Hey, they say.

I turn toward them. Are you—are you talking in your sleep?

Nope, they say. Are you?

I haven't really been sleeping.

Yeah, they say, about that.

I'm sorry am I keeping you up?

You and that spider. They point straight up to a large brown spider dangling halfway down over our heads.

Now I definitely won't sleep, I say, groaning into my pillow.

It's cool. We eat about eight of them a year on average.

Wow I hate that.

They prop their head up on their elbow. Did you know that spiders can tune their strings?

Tune how? I say.

They tell me: Like violin strings, they tune them to different frequencies so they can detect a predatory bird or a bat coming for them.

Whoa that's a lot. It's like, I'm not sure how people believe in god when spiders are right here doing engineering stunts like that.

So to you, these spiders disprove the existence of god?.

I just think their existence is more beautiful, I say.

But does that make a god any less true?

I'm pretty sure most people who believe in god don't believe in god because of truth but because god's a more beautiful idea to them.

So you're agnostic? they say, smirking.

No, I say. I'm tired. In every possible way.

———

In the morning we make waffles and head back to the museum a little while after it opens, and everything seems normal. As in, it doesn't seem like anything has been derailed because they discovered someone was in the museum or they've found a backpack full of human remains in one of the exhibition halls, et cetera.

Theo and I work out that they'll create some kind of diversion, at which point I'll slip into the back corner and grab B. Planning this gaff is the first time this experience has felt as cartoonish as it is, or cartoonish enough to alleviate some of the terror.

In the hammock forest, we both jump around a little bit trying to see if we can see the bag, and I catch sight of the open zipper pocket just before crashing into one of the bucket hat people. I realize I'm falling too late, and hit the iron bar that cordons off the diorama from the viewing area. People are rushing over to see if I'm okay, and I'm hurt but more a special excruciating blend of worried and humiliated: I'm wormiliated. Then I notice Theo emerging from the shallow woods with B on their back.

They mouth to me *you okay?* I stand up, throw my hands in the air, and announce that I got carried away because I was just so lucky to see fifty different plants and animals—FIFTY! Plants AND animals! The bucket hat people smile, and I do a weird curtsy and trot after Theo, who's already out the door and halfway to the museum exit. This is who I am: might as well use it for heists.

———

On our way out of town, we stop by Colclough Pond. It's the same sweet loamy gem in a quiet pocket of the wetlands.

Our first night in Gainesville, B and I came here after a few hours of curb scrounging, and we ate ice cream sandwiches while some local folks fished around us from the bank. B had a net with their research pack that we used to catch tadpoles. There were thousands, and the full surface of the pond moved with them. It looked like rainwater.

21

On our way up to Atlanta, I'm playing some of B's favorite songs that I made into a roadtrip playlist, which was Tina's idea. She said after her husband died, she took his iPod with her everywhere, sometimes listening to a song she didn't even like because she wanted to think about him singing it in the shower.

When B and I got together, it was the golden age of pop, and B was adamant about my music education, seeing as I'd grown up without any adults to impose their tastes on me and was fresh to the experience. FM did have a Dolly Parton's Greatest Hits cassette tape she would put on all the time at the airbrush shop, and when she stopped coming in after Ben left, I would listen to "9 to 5" over and over again feeling a glistening sense of indignation. Other than that and church hymns, B's music was my whole scene. I'm driving up 75 and Theo's crashed out in the passenger seat. B (less of B than before) is in the middle backseat, and my playlist is taking me back.

Stay Monkey (The Julie Ruin)
When Kathleen Hanna came back with The Julie Ruin, B was leaving Fran and New York to come back to Florida. They had been cool enough as a teenager to actually find Riot grrrl and use that punk meteor shower to fortify feelings the rest of us were still oblivi-

ous to or trying to hide. They were growing their hair back out. They were going to patch things up with their parents. They were helping Mr. Nguyen hang his new solo show at an upscale gallery that happened to be blocks away from the boardwalk where they would see a line of angry people lined up outside an airbrush shop. They were listening to this song just moments before they walked in and saved me. They said it was like my walk-on anthem.

When Doves Cry (Prince)

When B gave me Prince I went on a full bender: I fell asleep listening to my *Purple Rain* CD so much, my dreams for a whole year were spliced with heavy dancefloor fog machine synth. One time we drove down to Miami for an eighties-themed house party where people were downing mojitos two at a time and grinding on lawn chairs. By midnight B had stripped off their polyester and pleather skirt suit to do a backflip off the diving board. When they resurfaced, the first verse had started *dig if you will the picture*. They started singing and kind of swimming and dancing, and eventually everyone around the pool joined in. I remember them lounging naked on the pool stairs leading the party in song.

Heartbeats (The Knife/José González)

Somehow it never gets any less sweet: in the original version, it's like windowshopping in the middle of a stampede. In the acoustic version, it's much swishier, saleable: an advertisement for what exactly—parking lots at sunset? It's clear to me now that every image I conjure comes from the same mall in Gainesville where B and I went to buy a window AC unit because our place was the one apartment in the state without central air. We got there just as the stores were pulling down their gates, and ended up on the opposite end of the mall from where we'd parked. We had to walk through the whole place, eerily emptied and so florescent. From the speakers overhead we heard the growl of the synths and knew immediately what was playing. Then something swooped past our heads, and we looked around in a panic. Once more, a streak of something in the periphery. B said *oh my god it's a bat*, and we turned and saw it headed for us again and ran like hell. That bat followed us all the way to the entrance, hunting us to the tune of "Heartbeats."

On & On (Erykah Badu)

This lilting refrain looped through our lives over the years, returning at times with an ancient flavor, something preserved in amber—the way we can be surprised by something with no edges, no beginning and no ending. When B and I would get blue over long-distance communication or a string of long workdays, there was Badu for lullaby and dark revelation. When we would disappear to each other for a little while, this song would come through, its waves cresting.

Bidi Bidi Bom Bom (Selena)

Fran called B in the middle of their junior year finals to let them know that Selena had been killed, and they cried together for hours. Fran had just seen her perform the year before in New York for the *Amor Prohibido* tour. He learned that this song started out as "Bidi Bidi Bubbles" when Selena first improvised lyrics about a fish swimming out in the ocean, and then became a love song later. B and Fran listened to their favorite songs, taking turns playing them for each other over the phone, and lit candles for Selena. Years later, B and I attended a museum gala in Denver. At around nine, the live band retired for the evening and a DJ set up in the corner of the ballroom, kicking off the night with this legendary wah-wah bop. B teared up and led me to the middle of the floor, where we spun each other around for awhile.

(Nothing But) Flowers (Talking Heads)

B needed to take a research trip once to Jekyll Island in Georgia, and we went camping on a nearby island. It rained the entire time, but we made our own fun hiding out in the tent having sex and putting on shadow plays. One day we took a canoe out in the downpour and went into a natural tunnel under a landbridge that was so close to the surface of the water we had to bend all the way backward and lay flat with our backs on the canoe to make it through. There was something transformative about it: the experience took about four minutes but I came out on the other side feeling years older. Later we took mushrooms in the tent, and B told me they wished we'd known each other as kids, to which I said, *I don't know I think I was a pretty awful kid.* They said *wow I had no idea you still believed that.* Then they grabbed me and said *hey, I would have gotten held back one whole year in school just to hang out with you.* We played this song over and over again, and watched the treeline.

We Found Love (Rihanna)

For most of the time B was working in New York, they were staying with their sweetheart Nico, who did seventies glam drag and hosted a weekly lip syncing competition in Hell's Kitchen. Because Nico was a nightlife queen, B was getting up early to do detailed restoration work for one of the biggest museums in the world after nightlong warehouse parties. They were exhausted, but happy. When I came to visit, B was so wiped out they didn't even make it to Nico's show that night. I went to the show and nursed a beer by myself by the stage stairs. Afterward, Nico took me out in Brooklyn, and although we hadn't spent much time together before that, we had a gorgeous night. At dawn, someone put on *Talk that Talk* and we slowdanced to this song and thanked each other, and I had this new sensation of loving B by loving this person they loved.

All Is Full of Love (Björk)

When I first met B, they were working on rebuilding a relationship with their parents after living in exile with Fran. They weren't spending much time at home, but they would occasionally attend a church event, especially if it was a music night curated by B's mom, which meant Alvin would be there. B asked if I wanted to go to a Drum and Dance in the church basement, and apologized to me in advance. I thought they were joking, but they drove me to their family church and we went downstairs to a room where people were setting up chairs and taking hand drums out of bags. I met Alvin that night. We even shared a drum at one point. But the best part was when B and I took a long break from dancing and circled a food table between two mysterious lion sculptures in the Sunday School room, trying to get close to each other and the lions, showing off, telling our best jokes. When they took me home, this song was playing in their car, and we kissed each other without breathing for four minutes and thirty-two seconds.

22

IN ATLANTA, Highway 285 wraps around the perimeter of the city, cutting through the huge interstate Highways 75 and 85 across two axes like an inkblot. 285 blooms out with a bumper-to-bumper mélange of sprawl traffic day and night in the exact shape of white flight, with a big-box grocery store just on the outside of every curve. It takes us an hour to clear the traffic, and we stop at the Super 8 in the northeast part of the city.

We swim for a little just before the pool closes, and the only other people in the pool room are two kids who are busy throwing diving sticks for each other, and what looks to be their dad, who is really fixated on us. He glares right down at us for straight minutes without even turning his face out of discomfort when I make eye contact. Every now and then, he shakes his head a little. On our way out of the pool, I grab a towel from the hotel stack and make sure to scoot right past him. As I'm passing, I say *don't worry, you can't catch it.* Then I hold the glass door open for Theo and as they walk through, I squeeze their ass just once. They stifle a laugh and we breeze down the hall to our room.

Such a provocateur, they say.

We were making him uncomfortable anyway, thought we could at least have a little fun.

Do you feel like going out? they ask me.

Big day: can't be bothered, I say, but I am excited about cable. I turn on the TV.

Yeah, do you, says Theo. I think I'm going to go out. Is that okay?

Of course, I say.

No, really, they say. I could hang out with some cable.

Really. Go out, enjoy yourself. You know where to find me if you need anything.

———

I fall asleep lightning-fast. Theo creeps in a few hours later and goes right into the bathroom. I hear the shower turn on.

When they collapse into bed, I say hey, good night?

Oh yeah, they say. Actually lovely.

Are you drunk?

Nope.

Did you have sex?

Yup.

Aw, happy Atlanta! I say.

Happy Atlanta to us all, they say, and then we roll over and face opposite walls.

Night, I say.

They reach an arm behind and pat my thigh: night babe.

———

Theo drives the early morning leg, and I curl up all groggy and full of my dreams from the night before. In one dream, B speaks in that *Twin Peaks* garbled half-backwards talk, which they would love: I feel like at one point in real life they told me they would prefer to appear this way and that's why it's happening. Dreams are responsive to fantasy, but not in the way we expect.

In one dream B talks to me about some kind of wolf that the human body releases during sleep. This kind of wolf does not howl, but does perform cereal commercials from the nineties. I know this because B told me to look out for the one wolf that does Apple Jacks, which was my favorite cereal. I ask them what happened to the frog that used to do Apple Jacks commercials, and they say *cool melon pink baby*, so that's helpful. B also tells me the moon is looking for me, and then they ask me if I've forgotten. So I say, forgotten what, and they say: the human body, when did that happen?

I tell Theo all this, and they think for a minute, and then say: I'll bet you've been over there brooding trying to answer that question.

Wouldn't you be? I say.

No, you're not meant to answer the questions you ask yourself in dreams.

B asked me.

B is you, they say. Everyone in your dreams is you.

No, B is B. I say this with such force, Theo raises their eyebrows but doesn't say anything else. I start glitching with shame. My mouth is open, but nothing keeps coming out. I close my mouth with my hand and look down.

Theo turns on the radio, and *I Want To Break Free* is playing, and they say to me: you know this one?

Yeah, I say quietly.

Want to sing with me?

Yeah.

God knows, god knows, I want to break free.

23

JUST OUTSIDE LOUISVILLE, we pass a gigantic metal cross and a million rows of corn, which seem high for this time of year. Watching the corn pass relaxes my eyes. I ask Theo how they're doing because driving gets weird when there's a pattern like the lines on the road or this, and they tell me about how corn fields are the inspiration for visual white noise.

I am delighted to learn that pixels come from the doldrums of flyover country. It seems fitting that the American hearth should have such humble beginnings. I have always felt close to television because it is a portal out of this world, but also because it was my most stable connection, my family. Theo's mom and Tina didn't have TV until Theo was a teenager, so they are missing a whole nostalgic archive I rely on too heavily to connect with people, which makes for a lot of silence. But I trust the silence between us. We both seem consumed at times by our inner lives and content to be with ourselves side by side. When we're not singing or playing the one car game we made up where one of us says something and the other one says the first thing that comes to mind (no cheating), there are these long stretches when I work out how I'm feeling and their brain does something good for them too.

We stop at a rest stop to switch and stretch, and see a dirt road weave up through a cornfield to an old farmhouse. Right on the edge of the road facing the field is the scariest scarecrow I've ever seen in my life or in a movie or anywhere.

What the hell is wrong with that scarecrow? I say, unintentionally grasping Theo's shirt sleeve.

I think its face is missing.

Why! Why would they do that?

I'm not sure someone did that on purpose, Theo says, looking me over. They laugh.

What? I whine.

What are you so freaked out about?

This is exactly the kind of thing you always see in a horror movie because if it wasn't so dark it'd be silly. A nightmare trope. Something like that.

Maybe we should check it out.

———

I follow Theo up the dirt road toward the scarecrow, and finally we're close enough to see it really is a horror movie scarecrow because bees have built a hive in its hollowed out face. They are swarming around us, and I ask Theo if they think it's possible to read the scarecrows emotions from their movements like facial expressions, and Theo gives it a second and says:

Seems like as good a way as any to scramble facial recognition software.

Maybe one day we'll be able to order a face hive for that.

Reminds me of Samson's riddle, they say.

Oh no, is this a bible thing? I ask, moving away from the scarecrow back down the dirt road.

Yeah, but it's a rude one at least.

We slam our doors, and Theo pulls back onto the highway.

Okay, hit me, I say.

So Samson kills a lion with his bare hands. Then when he goes back he finds a beehive in the lion's carcass, and the bees are making honey.

That's pretty rude, I say.

Wait, that's not even the rude part. Later on, Samson is messing with some people and he tells them this riddle they can't know the answer to because it's based on this private memory of the lion and the beehive. So they guess for a bit, and then he eventually kills them for getting it wrong, and takes their shirts.

Super rude.

Yeah, so rude.

What's the riddle though?

Oh yeah, that's the best part, they say. "Out of the eater, something to eat; out of the strong, something sweet."

Oh that is good. You know what, Samson is just like Carl Akeley.

Who?

He was this eccentric taxidermy guy B used to talk about a lot. He did all the original taxidermy for dioramas at the Field Museum and the American Museum too—you'll see them. He basically changed how natural history museums taxidermied animals and displayed them with this special sculpting technique. He also influenced the landscape painters and foreground artists he worked with. B was obsessed with him.

Wow, I had no idea there was this secret cult of diorama artists.

This guy is definitely their god. He would go on these reckless hunting expeditions and get attacked by rhinos and always survive. He saw building museum dioramas as a conservation practice, like even if the animals were all gone from the wild, future generations could interact with a diorama the way we once interacted with animals in their habitats. In the epic diorama display that B restored called The Four Seasons, there are these white-tailed deer that were already endangered at the time Akeley killed and prepared a group of them for this particular exhibit. And meanwhile, he was going on safari with his wife and bringing back a bunch of elephants to stuff himself. It was a weird time for conservation.

Yeah, seems like the making of a natural history museum was never not going to be grotesque.

Especially under Akeley. But in the world of restoration he's a total legend. People love him.

Of course they do, says Theo. It's this whole Indiana Jones cowboy complex.

True, he is even described many places as "swashbuckling." Oh, and just like Samson, one time a leopard attacked him and he actually punched the leopard from the inside because his hand was already in the leopard's throat. Then he killed the leopard with his hands, and there's a famous picture where he's standing there in a sling gazing at this strung up leopard.

That can't be real. Punched from the inside?

Our very own biblical hero.

24

I'm burying B under those white-tailed deer because they're meticulous and B loved them. They used to point out how even the veins in their heads were carefully preserved by Akeley, how the fur was a little rough in places because that's what the snow would do. The gallery has been under construction all year for restoration work, but I saw on the website just before we left that visitors are invited back to the Nature Walk next weekend, so I'm a little worried we won't make it before they close the diorama cases again. I haven't decided which of The Four Seasons to bury B in, because Winter has the most ground matter to work with, but since I'll be burying B in snow in New York, I was thinking maybe Autumn. B loved the fall and we never get it in Florida.

———

In our room at the Grant Park Travelodge, we go over the plan. The Field Museum is not messing around with security. There are so many more alarms, guards, and complex entry and exit systems to deal with, I am exasperated before we even go in for our morning test visit. We buy a set of museum passes, which cost almost the same as Field Museum tickets, but get us access to the aquarium, the planetarium, and a free donut from Stan's. I like the idea of having access to the Shedd Aquarium, just steps away from the Field Museum, in case things get dicey and I need to hide out instead of following my escape route back into the city. Since The Four Seasons dioramas are on the Main Level, I can easily get to them and away from them using a number of stairwells and hallways. I won't be able to leave in the middle of the night this time. There is no way out until morning, which I'm trying to get excited about, since it was my childhood dream to live in a museum and sleep in the exhibit halls with Oreos and a hand radio. The safest places to hide all seem to be on the ground level, which means I would need to take a back stairwell to the diorama and back again undetected. There don't seem to be alarms on the doors, and fortunately The Field Museum is one of those monoliths where there are a lot of rooms like dark tunnels perfect for sheltering unsanctioned burials and whatnot.

The Nature Walk and Messages from the Wilderness exhibit is still under construction, with a tent of plastic sheets around the glass cases. I slip behind one piece of plastic to see if I can peer inside The Four Seasons. The Winter diorama had already been sealed, but the others are still open. I freeze in front of the Autumn diorama, where one deer stares directly back at me hauntingly, as if offering permission. I check myself, and remember that's probably what Akeley thought just before he bagged them up.

On the ground floor, we're checking out the rooms that will not be swept by security, like the lecture hall and the closed collections, and Theo has a revelation.

So there are a lot more guards here at every access point, right? they say.

Yeah, I'm worried, I say.

There are also a lot more people in other official roles who can give access but are not necessarily watching people in the same way.

There are docents, and exhibit staff, and whoever just kind of walking around in their little blazers.

Okay? I say. So, you're making me very nervous right now.

My point is human error. There are too many people with too many unclear roles around all the time being asked for directions and with their attention split everywhere. And most importantly, they say, look.

They point to a group of eager-looking teenagers receiving instructions from someone in a red blazer.

What am I looking at? I say.

Interns, they say. New summer interns. Theo holds out their phone. Look, it says the collections interns started this week.

They don't know what they're doing yet or their way around, they're nervous, and confused, and some of them have keys.

Sure enough, I look over, and a few of the interns are holding a key out in wonder like they were just told it would open a portal to hell.

Wow they really should not be giving these kids keys, I say.

I'm guessing one of those keys opens that door, says Theo, pointing to a room with a sign that says "Learning Collections: Closed for Summer Inventory."

That's your spot, they say.

You just have to find a way to get a key.

———

Theo and I go get lunch and jump in the lake for a few minutes. The water is glittery clear and endless over soft sand bars that recur five and ten and twenty feet out like there's no end to how many times you can start over. I did not realize how much love I could have for a cold lake. Back in the room, I put on my most inconspicuous tourist outfit. I have been saving a pair of oversized shorts for this moment.

Wait, I have something for you, says Theo, to complete the look.

They pull something out of their bag wrapped in tissue paper.

Ta-da, they say, and roll onto the bed laughing.

It's a bucket hat.

No, I say.

Come on, they say.

I will not bury B in a bucket hat.

You can take it off for the burial, they say, obviously.

25

ALL AFTERNOON I WANDER AROUND the museum pretending to be absorbed with insects or mummies or whatever, while I keep an eye out for where the interns are. I lose track of them when they go into collections areas off-limits for visitors, but they always seem to re-emerge from the same door a few minutes or an hour later. They eat lunch in the picnic area. They even all use the bathroom at the same time. I keep trying to figure out how in the world I'm going to get a key off of one of them to get into the Learning Collections area that Theo and I picked near the right stairwell.

It's getting close to the end of the workday, and people are leaving the museum en masse. I start to get frantic and start running, then realize I'm drawing attention to myself in a loony bucket hat no less, and I slow down. I sit by the sea mammals downstairs and breathe. I'm preparing myself to give up for the day and walk back to the Travelodge. I make one final pass across the Ground floor toward the movie theater, and do a double-take. There is a little gold key sticking out of the door to the Learning Collections area. It's just there.

I look up from the doorknob and see two interns walking toward me quickly with a big worried mood.

I turn the key in the lock, pull it out, and slip inside in one swift motion. I relock the door from the inside in the darkness.

Wait what? I hear one of them say. *It was right here. Shit, I left it right here. I was just down here. I can't believe this.*

Their shadows move the light around in the crack under the door.

Don't worry, I'll help you look. It's here somewhere.

I knew I was going to be the one to mess something up on the first day.

This probably happens all the time.

Do you think they're going to kick me out of the program?

No way, no. I mean, probably not.

———

Their voices trail off, and I'm alone. My eyes begin to adjust. The room is filled with miniature portable dioramas packaged like gifts ready to be shipped. Behind the back row, there is a good space to curl up and be out of sight should anyone open the door. I take inventory: B is secure in the army backpack. I have my phone but it's off so it can't accidentally go off and give me away. I also have a watch with a glow face that used to be B's. I have a little bit of water, a peanut butter crunch protein bar, and a combo knife with scissors, screwdriver, toothpick, and pliers. It's already after five, so the museum should be closed and all non-essential staff should be headed home.

I prepare for the six hours until I can go upstairs and do what I came here to do. For six hours, I will eat my protein bar incredibly slowly so it becomes an activity and a meal. I will think about my child self and how they would have wanted to use this time being in a museum overnight.

I inspect all of the miniatures, and feel like a god of this small world. I think about B and how much they loved this stuffy place. I imagine all the ways the museum's creatures could come to life and get themselves into trouble only to resolve everything and return to their exact places and poses when the museum opens. I will imagine B and I are also these creatures, and it is the others who do not belong here, not us. This is our museum. B and me: we're just more bodies, more dust, more objects at rest.

———

I don't mean to, but I doze off. I check my watch in a panic and am so relieved to find it's only eleven-thirty. I still have a window. I open the door a crack and look all around me. The lights are off, but the corridors are still brightly humming with exhibit lights, vending machines, emergency fluorescents, and other stray beams. I take a deep breath, and prance for the door to the stairs. All the lights are still on in the stairwell, and I feel exposed even though there's no one around. I hold the railing to steady myself, and climb. My body is shaking so much it's vibrating. I go up one flight and open the door just a bit, so I can see what the Main floor looks like. I am behind the Nature Walk, and the construction area is dim but visible. I do a kind of tiptoe to the plastic sheet nearest me. I go crazy for a half-second in anticipation of all the noise plastic makes, but I do one lifting motion, duck in, and release. The plastic makes a whoosh, but only one, and I remind myself that the sound could be just how things fall sometimes for no reason when they're left alone. I'm invisible. I'm nothing. I look at the white-tailed deer, and a wave of grief knocks me sideways. In the quietest whisper I can manage, I ask *do you remember B? They're right here.* I zip open the bag so slowly, I can feel the teeth pull apart one at a time. This is not the point of a zipper. I take B, and climb into Autumn, careful not to crush any of the leaves. B will have to go in the front, by the pond, by the deer that looks people in the eyes, where there is the most space for me to crouch. I dig the smallest hole with the pads of my fingers so there aren't any sharp edges, and lift B by the handful into this campy, sweet grave.

I don't remember walking away from The Four Seasons. I don't remember going down the stairs or back into the Learning Collections room. I do remember waking up in the back of the room in the morning, groggy and haunted by myself, my own existence in this dead place. This is happening. This is all real. I am doing this. I check my watch, and the museum has been open for twenty minutes. I wait another hour, drink some water, place the key on the floor by the door, and walk out the Ground floor exit of the museum, toward the water. I turn on my phone and call Theo.

I passed out at one but woke up at four and couldn't stop worrying about you, they say. How'd it go?

All according to plan, I say. I'm a pro now. And I'm exhausted.

Incredible, they say. Are you headed back here now?

Meet me at the Shedd, I say. I want to say hi to the alligators. I miss them.

Okay, they say. On my way.

———

At the alligator tank, Theo tells me they got a call from Tina this morning. The house is okay, but the hurricane wrecked her yard and my yard and half the neighborhood. She says she needs help cleaning up, and soon, because the plumbing is messed up and it's possible sewage might back up into one of our houses any minute now.

So what do we do? I say.

I think you have to keep going, they say. But I have to go back and help Tina. I can work on your yard too, empty the pool, and clean out the basement. You take the truck to New York.

But, I say, but I can't.

You were going to before I made you take me with you, and you can.

Okay, I know. You're just really good at scheming. You have good schemes.

I know, that's what I'm known for, they say.

So you're leaving?

I'm flying out of O'Hare tonight. We've already paid for one more night at the Travelodge, then you can leave for New York like we planned in the morning.

This is happening so fast, I say.

Fast as anything else, they say.

––––––

We head back to the Travelodge and Theo packs their bag. They leave me with the supplies, and I drop them at the Blue Line.

In the car, we put our arms around each other and kind of slump into each other until after a couple minutes Theo squeezes my sides.

Did you have a good time? I ask them.

The best, says Theo. The absolute best.

When they disappear behind the turnstiles, a new grief mixes with old grief in my body, and I'm out. I wander around the loop thinking about how there is too much world to know about that is so unconcerned with me, which is why I need B's good severe diamond eye—to watch for me and watch me. It took me so long to know myself, to begin living: how will I do it without them. To place just one part of my calf on just one part of their thigh again when we're sitting next to each other on the couch.

26

I WONDER IF NOW IS A GOOD TIME to have twelve hours to myself and long uninterrupted strips of asphalt on which to play out my life like a bad summer movie with lots of deleted scenes but not enough. At a rest stop in western Pennsylvania there are some Mennonites selling cinnamon rolls and other baked goods, and I buy a whole carload to have someone to talk to for fifteen minutes.

These young Mennonite women tell me that in their traditional culture, there's no dancing or television, but now their community allows them to have youth dances. They are thrilled about it because they do some fashion things for the dances too. They can only continue having the dances if they do line dancing specifically, so there's kind of a western theme to the fashion. They tell me they love bolos and boots. Anything structured is a good kind of dance, they say. Sometimes ballroom is okay too, but only the ones where you don't have to touch each other. They've been doing some dances that come from European courts and also some step dancing, and a little bit of choreo from Bollywood. They give me a free loaf of seeded bread and tell me to be careful in New York because they can tell I'm in a wounded way. I walk away from their stand and realize maybe this is one of those moments I've been talking to actual angels.

I figure when I get to New York, I can hand these breads out to folks on the street and have some more conversations. I realize this is exactly how Theo imagined me, in a place where I don't know anyone working out some new identity by losing myself in stranger stories. I get why this is not always a good thing, but I'm a landfill of memory right now.

I still have a lot more driving to go, so I'm trying to ignore this sharp pain in my throat, and my neck starting to get a little big in that way where I know I'm about to be fucked up by mucus. I just have to get to the Days Inn on the Upper West Side, and then I can wedge my head under a pillow and disappear into the sweaty void of sleep. Just as I'm finally rolling into the city, a fever sets in low around my eyes like those clouds that circle the mouth of a volcano. I grab some nighttime cold medicine from a Duane Reade and fall asleep spooning B in B's bag.

———

In the feverdream, B is inspecting the jaws of a lion. They walk around the museum: the museum we now live in, which is an amalgam of our house, all the places I have ever lived, and all the places I have buried and will bury B. The dioramas in this museum don't make any sense. They have the animals and some trees, but also, a toaster, a television, musical instruments, trash, mirrors, candles, beach umbrellas. The creeks have bath bubbles in them. There are rainbow streamers in the back of a diorama with hyenas. There is bunting that says 01101000 01100001 01110000 01110000 01111001 00100000 01100010 01101001 01110010 01110100 01101000 01100100 01100001 01111001. I can't read it but I can hold it in my head, which feels like another kind of understanding. There are windows in the back of some of the dioramas, where people seem to be washing dishes in a kitchen. One diorama has a hotel bed in it. This hotel bed I'm in right now. One diorama has a bird in a cage, which I point to, and shout to B:

Seems like overkill!

Huh? they say. Roadkill?

They move from diorama to diorama like they are looking for something. They stick their hand in a lion's mouth, and shake their head, *no, that's not it.* They approach an alligator, and place their hand in the long jaws of the alligator. They pull it away and shake their head again. They do the same with a grizzly bear. They appear to be getting more and more frustrated. I try to help them, but they ignore me. Finally, they place their hand in a wolf's mouth, and their face changes. They get so excited they jump in the air. They run to me and bring me over to the wolf to introduce us.

This is the one, they say.

I'm trying to match their enthusiasm, but I don't understand.

This is the one I've been wanting you to meet, they say to me.

Okay, I say.

I'm not sure what's happening. The wolf doesn't move or speak. I look at B to try and figure out what they want.

What do you want me to do? I say.

Come on, says B, taking my hand.

They put my hand in the paw of the wolf.

I want you to be happy, they say. Both of you.

———

I wake up soaked in sweat and groan. Today is supposed to be my test visit at the museum, but I can't imagine leaving this bed right now. I look at my phone screen and worry I am hallucinating because I have a message from Fran. I've been trying to reach him for what feels like forever. I feel no relief. I'm furious about the returned call because it feels so late. In real time it's only been a few weeks, but in grief time, he has left me out here on my own for lifetimes. I don't know if I have it in me to listen to the message, but Fran needs to know about B, and I could use some family right about now.

I get myself out of bed, take a hot shower, and manage to get outside into the sunlight. There's something about Manhattan that is so hot and smelly and crowded and brimming, you actually find this weird peace. The cold medicine makes me feel floaty over the highway and the Hudson, and I sit down in Joan of Arc Park in Riverside and listen to Fran's message.

He apologizes, a lot. He was on a retreat in the Cape with no service. I'm annoyed, but now more grateful than anything to hear his soft-spoken baritone, his almost imperceptible habit of going up at the end of every sentence like everything is a question, a wondering, a curiosity. Good old Fran. He'll be wrecked.

I call him back to let him know I'm in New York, sick, and in the middle of a scheme that is so beyond any of my other schemes, he would be proud. I tell him we need to talk about something, today if possible. He demands I leave the hotel and come stay at his so he can make me an essential oil cleanse and some sopa de fideo.

That sounds great, but this scheme is a lot, Fran, I say. I could get in real trouble. You sure you want me at your place?

Baby, what's changed, he says. We've always been against the law.

Okay, I'll head over in a few hours.

So why didn't B make the trip up with you? Are they busy with work? he says.

I've been dreading this moment.

No it's not work, I say. Hey I have to go, but we'll talk when I see you later!

Okay, love you baby, he says. Can you pick up some chicken thighs on the way?

Yeah, love you, I say.

———

I hang up the phone and call Theo. I miss how they're easy to be around and also completely stubborn and also up for anything. They've been staying at Tina's cleaning and doing handy things. I let them know about being sick and delayed and hearing from Fran. They drained the pool, they tell me. My plants must love a hurricane because the everything in the yard is suddenly growing like crazy. The house is good. Almost no flooding, they report. I ask them about the dishwasher.

Run it for me, will you, I say.

Sure. Let me know when you get out of this one safe, they say. Full moon in Capricorn tomorrow.

27

WHEN I OPEN THE DOOR TO FRAN'S, he doesn't rise from the couch, but rather beckons me to him. He has these small ways of making me feel like I live here and just haven't been home in awhile. He wraps his arms around me and asks me about my plans in the city. He puts his hand to my forehead as if to feel for my temperature and then strokes my cheek. He asks me if I'm having a sad summer. I feel raw. I nearly collapse at his knowing.

We cook up the chicken thighs and let the soup simmer, and Fran shows me his new Kiki Smith print. It's an etching of what looks to be the bottom of a squid, and a little bit larger, just below, a spider with a flower on its thorax. It's called *Untitled (for David Wojnarowicz)*. Fran met Kiki and David in the late eighties and modeled for some X-rays they were working on. He and David had a summer fling, nothing too serious, but mostly, David's influence changed Fran's work forever. They were collaborators and friends. David and Fran shared a birthday, and one year held a joint rooftop celebration that they both documented on film the whole time. They left the party to drink gimlets and compare and cut their shots together. Fran left New York for Mr. Nguyen's when David died. B used to say, *David is Fran's Fran.*

Fran asks if I'm planning to get to the museum while I'm here, which makes me wonder if his intuitive magic has bloomed to an intolerable power, or if there is such a thing as bleak coincidence. It's so good to talk to Fran, I forget for a moment that he doesn't already know about B, and that he will soon have to feel that rupture. We sit down at the table to eat, and I'm panicked. I'm straining against this thing I have to do, when Fran says:

Okay Jules, what's going on?

Fran, I start. I put a burning spoonful of broth in my mouth and shut my eyes tight.

What is it, says Fran.

Fran, there was an accident. B hit their head, and the hospital, they weren't able to stop the bleeding. B died a few weeks ago.

No, no, what? Fran says quietly. How—how did—

He looks at me, and I just nod.

Then he shouts no, and hits the table with both hands so hard soup spills out of both our bowls. He stands up, knocking over his chair, and disappears into his bedroom.

I give him a few minutes, and then push the door open to find him lying on his bed with his face in a pillow sobbing. I hold him, and I cry too, and finally: to mourn with someone else who knew and loved B is such a gift.

———

When B was working at the Ameican Museum, Fran got a pass and visited all the time. He would show up and take them out for lunch, or pick them up at the end of the day because there was some kind of protest or party or Fran had something to tell them that couldn't wait. He knew the museum and eventually the history better than many of the docents, and would interject when he overheard an error in the tour.

He was devoted to B's work, and he let them use his studio to experiment with chemicals and materials to produce the airbrushed marble dust that would become their signature in diorama foreground restoration. In that way he is present in the dioramas B worked on at the museum, and in everything they made. And whenever they would feel themself losing direction, as Mr. Nguyen taught them, they would pay tribute to Fran.

Fran was paying tribute to Mr. Nguyen and David Wojnarowicz, who was paying tribute to Arthur Rimbaud, and Peter Hujar, who he called "the wind in the air." Hujar was paying tribute to Diane Arbus, who was paying tribute to outsiders and queers and radical artists, who were willing to be photographed, so B would know generations later they were alive in their discomfort and resilience. B paid tribute to all these artists, and B made things that led them to me, and then B let me know I was alive in my discomfort and resilience, which is how I made it this far.

28

I TELL FRAN EVERYTHING. I tell him about B's family, what happened at the hospital. I tell him about Alvin's weird way of trying to include me after the funeral, and I show him what's left of B in the army backpack. He says he's sorry and holds me some more. It's sad but not surprising.

Right, I say, which is another thing to be sad about.

In death, Fran says, we are the most valuable because we can't disprove their narratives. So B is a saint, and you, well. If they can make us invisible while we're still alive, queer death proliferates. It recolors the world.

So this is only—what's a third of two-thirds?

I don't know, says Fran. I don't do math.

This is only that much of B.

Wow, fuck. Fran places his hand over his heart and stares at the bag. Where's the rest?

That's my scheme, I say. That's why I'm here, to bury B.

Oh, says Fran. Where?

I've been breaking into museums, Fran, I say.

Oh my god, he says. His lips curl into a dark little smile. Oh no, not the American Museum.

Yes. Tomorrow.

You'll never get in there. You'll never get out!

I have to, I say. I'll find a way. I open my other bag, and start to unfurl my museum maps. So the wolf diorama is being restored again because of the new lighting. They're using B's technique for the moon shadow on the snow: I read about it. The glass is down right now, and the whole area should be cordoned off.

Well, you've certainly done your homework, Fran says. He seems genuinely impressed.

What I don't know, I say, is the guard schedules, and I don't know what the alarm system is like, but that's easy enough to figure out when I go in.

Wait, Fran says. He runs both hands through his hair. Wait! He is running in little circles around the table. Wait wait wait wait!

What?

What if you don't have to break in.

Oh yeah, I've already figured that out. I've been going during open hours and then finding places to hide, so I only really have to break out.

No I mean, what if you could do it without having to hide or break out.

I don't follow.

I know everyone there. I mean, last year I dated this sweet guy who's a security guard there, Remy. Sometimes we still see each other. I could explain the situation to him—maybe he'll understand. He could walk us back there.

Wait, what's this us? No, Fran. I'm not dragging you into this.

You're hardly dragging me, Fran says, I'm in.

Nope, I go in alone.

His face drops. Please, he says.

We'll see. If you can get Remy on board, then okay.

I'm just going to make a quick phone call, he says. He dials his cell, and then while still holding eye contact with me, he says, *hey baby, you working tomorrow?*

29

FRAN AND B AND I WALK through Central Park for the first time in years. The leaves shimmy on the branches and splash light all around us. Fran takes my hand.

Breathe, he says.

You're pretty good, you know that Jules?

I guess, I say. On my better days.

Your only problem in the whole universe is that you forget to breathe.

And what's your problem, I say.

My problem is that I love too much, says Fran, completely deadpan. Then throws his head back and sighs.

Times like these I really can't tell if he's making a joke or trying to be profound or being profound by trying to make a joke.

What was B's problem?

He looks at me and grins. Too much glue, he says. Always too much glue.

———

Remy is waiting for us where the museum tours start, right in front of the Hall of North American Mammals. Fran introduces us, and

Remy takes my hand with both of his hands and tells me he's sorry about B. He says he didn't know them, but the exhibitions people talk about them all the time. He'll be right here, he says, guarding from the Central Park West entrance, but before we go in, a couple things:

The Hall of North American Mammals is so central, this will be difficult to pull off. Even if you're able to get into the diorama, there's always someone around—it's risky.

He rotates to the second floor at 12:30 so we only have a half hour on his watch. He's not typically in this area, so he doesn't know what the traffic has been like for people working on the restoration.

Fran owes him one Manhattan and the whole story, to be collected at a later date.

Good luck.

Just like that, Fran and I walk right into the Hall of North American Mammals at the American Museum of Natural History in the broad light of day. I don't have to break into anything. I don't have to fight or wait or hide. We approach B's favorite diorama in the museum, and are relieved to find that the glass is still set to the side. "Wolf" is an understated nearly hundred-year-old winter scene of two wolves running at night in northern Minnesota. In the moonlight, the wolves' blue shadows stretch out over the snow. We crouch down to touch B's fake snow. Fran and I each place one hand on the snow. Part of me expects cold, and a shiver runs through my body in anticipation. We look at each other. There are tears in Fran's eyes. The snow is made of crushed, colorized marble. It is not white, but grayish indigo, opaque but with sparkle. I realize that digging a hole in this snow might be more difficult than it was in the dirt foreground of Autumn diorama at the Field Museum.

Fran and I brought a few kitchen items that might be better than our hands: we have a wooden spoon, a metal ladle, a small plastic cup, a miniature trowel, and a coffee scoop. The coffee scoop seems to be the best bet, so very carefully, I scoop a little of the snow near the few thin trees on the right side of the diorama. The scoop is not working, the marble dust sifts and replaces itself immediately. Next I try the trowel. The snow is colored for the shadow cast by the moon so carefully, and I'm trying to only move the base color of marble snow aside. It's taking longer than we'd planned. I look at my watch, and it's already almost 12:30. Fran offers to go check with Remy, but I tell him we can't risk going back out and in like that.

That's when we hear the footsteps. My chest lurches. Before I can even turn to Fran, there's a voice.

What's going on here?

Fran and I turn at the same time. He is standing, and I'm on my knees. I can barely stand from nerves. I manage to pocket the trowel while turning, but we look guilty anyway.

What are you doing? A tall man in khaki shirt and pants is waiting for us to say something. I'm trying to figure out the best lie, when Fran steps toward the man.

Oh my god, he says, Jeff? It's Fran! I didn't know you were still here.

The man (Jeff, presumably) now looks at us with recognition and new slightly different kind of confusion. I'm not, he says. I'm just back to work on this project with some of the new artists. But what—what are you doing in here?

So, Jeff, do you have a minute? So good to see you.

Fran puts his arm around Jeff and walks him away from me. He turns back to me and says: Jules why don't you grab something from the cafe. I'll meet you there.

I mouth to him *what's going on*, and he does this fast nod thing and smiles to say he's taking care of it. I don't know what's happening, but I take B to the cafe and leave them. I'm wracking my brain trying to figure out what the situation is, how Fran knows this Jeff; but nothing I can imagine makes this okay. I'm thinking about the time B told me their favorite thing about working at the American Museum is that all the curators and artists were gay. At the time, I was bitter about being stuck in Florida, so I didn't give a lot of thought to what a sweet work environment that must have been for B. I also kind of assumed all of New York was gay and I was missing out on that.

I see Fran and Jeff wandering around the exhibits chatting and pointing at things. Fran waves at me. I'm stunned by whatever casual hang out has popped up in the middle of our crime.

Fran and Jeff make their way over to me all chummy, and Jeff sticks out his hand.

Wow, he says, such a pleasure to meet you.

Uh, what? I say. I mean, you too.

Jeff was B's boss, Fran says to me. They restored that wolf diorama together. Jeff and I got to know each other because I'd be picking B up at five, and it was always *one more thing, one more thing.* They would keep working until Jeff was basically pushing them out the door.

Ah, I say. B could be that way about their projects, especially if they were doing something they'd never done before.

Right, says Fran. Kind of a perfectionist, but a fun one.

I'm so sorry to hear about B, Jeff says. They were absolutely brilliant. They were, he stops. Well you know. Fran told me about what you're doing.

I suddenly feel very exposed. I feel shame like a fluttering around my neck. I look angrily at Fran.

Don't worry. It's okay, says Fran.

Jeff looks at Fran and then me. I want to help, he says. B and I made that snow together. I'm probably the only one who can move it and not injure the diorama.

I feel like I'm dreaming. Now I don't have to break in or hide, and there is a trained professional who wants to help me bury B. I've come a long way since Chicago. I start to cry without realizing it, and Fran hands me his handkerchief.

Let us help you, he says.

Okay, I say.

———

Jeff, Fran, and I walk back into the Hall of North American Mammals. Jeff moves the crushed marble with what look like surgical tools so carefully it takes him almost an hour to create a hole deep enough for B. We each take a turn pouring a little bit of B, and then Jeff replaces the moved marble, brushing the edges and checking the color placement with three different lights. We stand in front of the diorama, and I know we've given B one hell of a funeral.

At home in their favorite paradox: these wolves run in this snow for years and never get wet. They never get cold. They're dead and will never die. Now B would go on this way. What a strange way to worship what we find most beautiful about our world. These creatures something more than dead and yet ready to perform. Everything back from dust when it is called.

30

WE HUG JEFF AND THANK HIM. Fran and he make plans to catch up. It feels like we've had this completely normal, if emotional, day together. We see some of the new exhibits because we can. What a revelation, to be just another museum visitor. In Birds of the World, Fran asks me if I'll stay with him awhile longer. He's tired of living alone and it could be good for me. I tell him I have to return the truck and spend some quality time with my dishwasher. But I'm thinking I'll come back and stay at Fran's after that. I might want to live in New York, where everyone is gay and people show up to help you bury the love of your life.

On our way out of the museum, Fran walks me by a gallery on the First floor called the Gottesman Hall of Planet Earth (H.O.P.E).

I wanted to show you this, he says.

It's nice, I say. I start to read the gallery text.

No, not because of what's here now. Because of what it is.

Tell me, I say.

This is where they filmed it, the moon landing.

I look around at the room, dark except the glow of the installa-tion panels.

Can you imagine it? he says. This room is the moon.

––––––––

I close my eyes and open them. I imagine the lunar rover. I imagine the astronaut suits, the smart material and the way it holds up in simulated zero gravity. The artists standing by to touch up moon rocks and arguing about the way the flag would blow but not blow when they stick it in the ground. I imagine Mr. Nguyen consulting on film speed, and then sitting down to roll a bunch of cigarettes be-fore the next take. I imagine Americans sitting in their living rooms, watching the grainy moon on their TV screens like it's god's own buzzcut, and they want to touch it. But not with their hands: with that fathom in them that's a cool null too. We did it: we landed on the moon. We used to be so afraid of space but now, look at it up there. The whole blessed void: a vast field of care.

ABOUT THE AUTHOR

RE Katz is a former Artist in Residence at Dreamland Arts and Women and Children's Hospital of Buffalo. They are the author of *Pony at the Super* (Horse Less Press, 2015). They work in educational justice in Chicago and are interested in personal fashion, antifascist witchcraft, and television.